FINDING LIMITS

A CORRUPT COWBOYS STANDALONE

EMMA CREED

Finding Limits
Copyright © 2024 by Emma Creed
All rights reserved
First Edition

Editing by: Sassi's Editing Services
Proofreading and formatting by: Andrea Stafford

AUTHOR NOTE

Warning

Finding Limits, and all books in the Corrupt Cowboys series are works of fiction and contain adult content. Due to the nature of the series you should expect to come across various subject matter that some readers may find disturbing, and it is intended for readers 18+

Please contact the author if you have any questions.

emmacreedauthor@gmail.com

WHATEVER IT TAKES

Six Months Ago

"Good to see ya." My old friend, Jimmer Carson, greets me with a slap on the back as I step into the foyer of the Dirty Souls MC clubhouse.

"I appreciate ya gettin' here so quick." He tips his head at me gratefully.

"Only for you." I shrug, following him through the foyer to a door on the right that leads down some narrow steps toward a basement.

"This ain't the way we usually treat our guests but...this one's a little different." He stops in the corridor and turns to face me with a concerned look on his face.

"Mitch, I'll warn ya before we go in there. This girl... she's been to hell and back." His voice lowers to a whisper as he scratches his beard. "She's Skid's old lady's sister, and she's been kept in some filthy bunker by the cult leader Addison ran away from."

"Cult?" I stare back at him. "Didn't those kinda things dry out in the seventies?"

"This ain't no Charlie Manson shit, Mitch. I can't even begin to tell ya what shit those fuckers were preachin'."

"And this cult, I'm assumin' they've been dealt with?" It

seems a stupid question, I've known Jimmer Carson for a lot of years and he never does half jobs, but I like to cover all bases.

"Of course, but for this girl, I'm afraid the damage is done. Her sister got out five years ago, but the husband she ran away from took all his grievances out on her little sister when she left. He's beaten her every day since as a punishment. Kept her chained in that bunker like a dog, you can imagine what that's done to her head." He frowns.

"*Jesus.*" I shake my head.

"So what are we supposed to do for her back in Fork River?" I move on to the reason I'm here. If Jimmer wants me to take this girl, I need some kind of clue on what to do with her.

"She can't heal around Addison, she's still got all those beatin's drummed inside her head, sometimes she chants the words he said to her. We need to get this girl away from her sister until she's feelin' better. It's breakin' Addison's heart, but we all agree it's what's best. She needs time to adjust to a normal life. Somewhere she can ease into gently. Somewhere off grid, and quiet."

"You ever known Fork River to be quiet?" I raise an eyebrow at him.

"Well no, but my nephews have got it handled, and I know there are people I can rely on there," he points out, and I nod my head in agreement. We all wear the Carson brand to prove it.

It's been good watching Jimmer and his nephews get closer over the past few years. Jimmer's brother, Bill, always resented him and the life he chose over the ranch, but since Bill's death, the bond his sons have made with their uncle has become solid.

"I've had Maddy look into some shrinks in your area, we'll organize all that and fund it, but for now she just needs to be taken care of. It's not gonna be an easy road for her. She hardly talks, she's afraid of her own shadow. But with some patience and understandin', I think she can get better." Jimmer looks hopeful, reminding me that despite the brutality he's capable of, he's got a good heart inside that strong chest of his.

"I'm sure the girls back home can be all those things for her." I smile back to reassure him. Maisie, Leia, and Savannah are all good women, and they're not just kind, they're strong. It sounds to me like they're just what this poor little wretch needs.

"Come." Jimmer turns and walks toward the door at the end of the corridor.

"So, why ya keepin' her down here? Didn't ya say she was locked in a bunk—"

"It's where she seems most comfortable. Everythin' beyond this room seems to trigger her." He shrugs sadly before he opens the door.

At first glance, the girl I see resembles a scolded child. She's sitting in the corner of the cold, damp room with her arms wrapped tight around her knees. Her hair is cropped short and uneven and her bony arms are covered with bruises.

"Everleigh." Jimmer approaches her with caution.

"I want you to meet a friend of mine." He crouches down, leaving a respectable gap between the two of them. The girl doesn't look up, she just keeps rocking herself and staring at her feet.

"His name is Mitch and he comes from the town that I grew up in, Fork River. It's in Montana and it's real beautiful there, darlin'." He looks up at me and smiles sadly. "It's quiet and it's the perfect place to do some healin'." He keeps his tone soft, so soft that I almost forget who he is and what he's done over the years.

"I need ya to trust this man the same way you've trusted me. I give you my word that he won't hurt ya."

The girl says nothing, just slides herself up the wall so she's standing. She looks so small and fragile, I can't understand how any man could have gotten his kicks outta hurting her.

"Pleased to meet ya, Everleigh." I take off my Stetson and lower my head, and when her eyes flick up to meet mine, I'm immediately struck by how blue they are. Her eyelashes bat wildly as she stares at me for what seems like minutes and I feel something inside me shift.

"Jimmer's right, darlin', I may look scary but you got my word that I won't hurt ya." I hold out my hand for her to take and when I step forward she flinches back against the wall.

"She won't be touched," Jimmer tells me, lifting a bag off the camp bed that's in the corner of the room. "The girls here all pulled together and packed her some clothes and essentials. I take it you've got the cabin ready?" he checks

"It's gonna need some work, but it's livable," I assure him. The old safe house Jimmer's father, Hank, built on the ranch's land hasn't been maintained for years.

I notice the way Everleigh looks at Jimmer, desperate and helpless. She doesn't want to come with me, she doesn't understand that all this is for her own good. And why should she? Five years locked in a bunker, being beaten and God knows what else would cause anyone to lose their faith in humanity.

"Darlin', I can't keep you locked up down here, it ain't good for ya. The world's waitin' for ya out there, and I know you're scared, but I can promise that the worst has already happened. Let Mitch take ya to the Copper Ridge ranch. There ain't no place like it. You can look for miles without seein' another buildin', and the sunsets are perfect. You've spent far too long starin' at walls. Go, be free."

She nods her head and smiles ever so slightly. Then when she turns to me she takes a brave breath and allows the smile on her face to grow a little wider.

The girl is so weak she can't make it all the way up the stairs without stopping to take a breath, but we're patient, and I remind myself not to touch her when she has to press her hand against the wall for support.

When we eventually make it outside, I open the door of my truck for her to get in the passenger seat and she just about manages to pull herself up. Jimmer hands her her bag through the window and she smiles at him gratefully.

"You gotta long ride home. Will ya make a stop off?" he asks me as I get into the driver's seat.

"Nah, I stopped at a motel a few miles back and got my head down for a few."

"A motel?" Jimmer looks offended. "You know you could've stayed here."

"C'mon, we both know there wouldn't have been much sleepin' goin' on if I'd stayed here." I wink as I get myself behind the wheel.

"Good luck." Jimmer nods at us both, and I salute him before taking another look at the girl who's so beautifully broken I wanna be the one to fix her.

I wait until I get outta Manitou Springs before I make any attempt to have a conversation with her. I can see she's nervous by the way her eyes keep flicking across to me and how her hands are shaking as they cling to the bag on her lap.

"So, ya lookin' forward to seein' Montana? Jimmer's right, it's beautiful there." I keep my eyes on the road and when she makes no attempt to answer me, I figure I need to try a little harder. "You're gonna love the girls that Jimmer's nephews are shacked up with. You'll get on well Maisie, she's Garrett's wife, and they have triplets together. Two boys and a little girl. Then ya got Leia, who's with Wade, they got a little one on the way too. Maisie's friend, Savannah, can be a little wild, but she's good fun and I'm sure it's only a matter of time before Cole pulls his finger outta his ass an—"

"Are you my master now?" The girl interrupts me with a quiver in her tone.

"*Your what?*" I almost crash the damn truck, and when I quickly pull over and turn to face her, she looks petrified by my reaction.

"You listen to me, where I'm takin' ya there are no masters. There are no bunkers or beatin's and the only god you have to believe in is the one you decide to make ya peace with." I don't mean for my words to come out so harsh, but seeing this girl so fragile and afraid makes me pissed that the fucker who hurt her is already dead. I'da really liked to have taught the bastard a few lessons of my own.

Despite how stern I am, Everleigh seems to take in my words, closing her eyes and nodding, then with a relieved, little sigh that sounds all kindsa beautiful she rests her head against the window and goes to sleep.

———

"Home sweet home." My eyes are heavy when I eventually pull up outside the cabin, Everleigh is the opposite. She's bright and alert as she stares at the space around her in complete awe.

"Jimmer wasn't lyin' when he said you won't see anythin' for miles." I chuckle as I get out the truck and move around to hold the door open for her. I've driven all night and straight through to morning because I didn't want to put the girl through a stop off. I'm assuming this is a big enough transition for her as it is.

"Ya smell that?" I inhale deep as I stretch out my back. "That's fresh, early, Montana air. It's good for ya." I give her some space so she can get out the truck and when I offer to carry her bag for her she shakes her head and keeps it clutched to her chest.

"Now, I'll warn ya, this place ain't nothin' fancy, but the roof don't leak, it's got runnin' water, and somehow the electric wires are still workin'." I lead her onto the porch, almost knocking my head on the oil lamp that's hanging from the rafter.

"Fuckin' thing." I rub the back of my head and when I see the slight hint of a smile on her lips, it automatically causes one of my own.

"Glad you found some amusement in that." I clear my throat before I open the door for her and when she steps inside, I watch as her eyes slowly take everything in.

"Kitchen's over here, I had Josie, Garrett's housekeeper, stock the fridge. The TV works but ya ain't got all them fancy channels." I point over to the living area. "There's a bedroom through here." I step across the floor and open the door. "Ya can put your bag right here on the bed." This time when I go to take it from her she lets me.

"I'll organize someone to get you a phone so you can call me if ya need anythin' and I'll check in on ya every day—"

"No." Suddenly those pretty, blue eyes grow wild with panic, and she shakes her head.

"Jimmer said you'd take care of me." I notice that her chest is rising and falling far too quickly.

"And I will, darlin', I—"

"You can't leave me out here by myself. It's too exposed. What if he finds me?"

"Sweetheart, from what I heard, the man who hurt you is dead. He can't—"

"They can't be dead. God wouldn't allow it. He needs them." I don't know what she's talkin' about but when I automatically go to comfort her she steps back and knocks into one of the chairs behind her. It startles her and when she screams I hold up both my hands to assure her that I won't touch her.

"Calm down. It's just a chair. You're safe here," I tell her. Jimmer wasn't bull-shitting. This girl really is messed up.

"You can't leave me." She shakes her head frantically. "You can't leave me out here all alone." Her eyes fill up with tears and I feel her pain as if it's my own.

"Okay. Okay, I'll stay." I move slowly, managing to get a little closer.

"Promise?" she whispers as those tears spill from the corners of her eyes and roll down her cheeks. She's so pretty and it makes the urge to wipe them away hard to hold back.

"I promise. I'll stay right here. I'm not gonna let anythin' happen to you, Everleigh. And no one's comin' for ya. There ain't no one left to come."

CHAPTER 1

MITCH

Present Day

I wake up with a start when I hear her screams. Screams that sound as if she's being split open and pulled inside out. It puts a pain in my own chest when I'm reminded that there's nothing I can do to make it better.

It's been six months since Everleigh came here, six months of me sleeping on this damn couch and six months of me listening to her relive all those horrors of her past without being able to comfort her.

I throw off my blanket and get up from the couch, heading toward her door then sliding down it onto my ass and resting my head back against it.

"Everleigh. You're dreamin', darlin'," I call out, hoping that she'll hear me. I can't go in there when she's in this kinda state. I learned that lesson on the first night I spent here with her. She damn nearly clawed the skin off my flesh when I tried to wake her. Not that it bothered me, I'd take her scratches every night of the week if it meant I got to hold her. They ain't what keep me on the other side of this door during her terrors. It's the fear that I saw in her eyes, and knowing that during that split second, she thought I was her monster. I never wanna see that again.

"Everleigh! You ain't there no more," I yell out again, needing her to hear me. I can't stand the thought of her being back at that place and reliving whatever she's been through, over and over. I wanna smash through the door and scoop her up tight in my arms, and the frustration of being unable to builds up inside me and makes me wanna hurt somebody.

All this anger and pain is confirmation of what I've been trying to avoid since she came here. The last thing I want to admit is that I've grown a fondness for the pretty, broken girl that Jimmer sent here to heal. She may not have made much progress, and she still barely speaks a word, but every morning she gives me a smile over the breakfast table that sets me up for the day I got ahead of me.

Life for me has changed a helluva lot since she came here. I pretend that I'm okay since we lost Dalton a few months ago, but I ain't. I see his face every time I close my eyes. I think of all the things I had left to teach him and I beat myself up constantly for the way I let him down. That boy had a heart too kind for this world, and it was that heart that got him killed.

The ranch is too busy for me to lose myself, especially now that Garrett has become Fork River's new mayor. And as much as I'd like to lock myself away in this cabin with Everleigh and pretend the rest of the world don't exist, I force myself each day to push on. It's what Dalton would do.

I'm wise enough to know that it's not healthy for me to feel this way about the girl. She's far too young for me, and although her progress is slow, it's bound to happen one day. Then, just like a baby bird, she's gonna wanna fly from the safety of this nest. It's something I try to remind myself of every time I look at her. But right now, she's here, and I can't help but appreciate everything about her, even all those broken pieces that may never get fixed.

"The Lord shall punish," she starts to chant, and I look up

at the ceiling and sigh. I stopped trying to picture what the fuckers in that cult might have done to her. All it does is make me rage, and rage is not what Everleigh needs around her. She needs calm, she needs peace, and I want so badly to be the one who gives her all that.

"Everleigh, you ain't there no more, darlin'," I call out over her cries, swallowing the large lump that's wedged in my throat. "Follow my voice, wake yaself up for me." That pain just keeps on splitting me open, making it harder and harder for me to stay on this side of the door.

The screaming abruptly stops, and all that can be heard are desperate breaths that tell me she's coming out of it. "That's right, you leave all that behind, and come back to me," I coax her back to a world where she's safe.

"Mitch." Hearing my name whisper from her lips makes me smile to myself.

"I'm right here, darlin', right here," I assure her, keeping that smile on my face as I imagine her nestling her head back into her pillow and taking comfort in the fact she knows I'm just the other side of this door.

"Thank you." Her voice comes out so weak I barely hear it but I still feel it's warmth in my chest

"Anytime," I manage, before closing my eyes and letting myself fall back to sleep.

"Mornin'." I lift up my hat when Everleigh comes outta the bedroom. She stops and stares at me in both shock and horror when she realizes that I'm cooking breakfast.

"I should—"

"You sit yaself down. You've done breakfast every mornin' since ya been here. I figured it's my turn." I pull out a chair for her and ignore how uneasy she looks about the entire situation. I've spent the past six months allowing her to do things her way. She keeps this place immaculately clean, she prepares every meal we eat, and she does all the laundry. I'm guessing it's what the women, back where she came from, were expected to do, and I decided last night that this girl ain't ever gonna heal if she don't get pushed outta her comfort zone.

She sits with her back straight and a nervous look on her face as her eyes watch me plate up the turkey rashers and scrambled eggs that I've made us.

"Here, I'll bet it don't taste as good as yours, but it's nice to have breakfast made for ya, ain't it?" I've learned that over the past six months, too. Her breakfasts sure beat the shit that gets rustled up in the bunkhouse.

"Tha...Thank you." She forces a smile at me as I place a plate in front of her, then I take the space opposite her with my own.

I watch on as she links her fingers and bows her head, and after she's whispered her prayers she looks up at me and smiles awkwardly. I never join her in her prayers, I lost faith in the man upstairs when he took my nephew from me, and I'm sure she thinks I'm going to Hell for it.

I won't tell her that the sins I'll be going to Hell for are a lot darker than forgotten prayers.

I watch her take each bite of what I made for her, feeling a lot like I accomplished somethin'. With Everleigh, any step forward seems like a huge achievement, it's not something that happens often.

"You got Samantha comin' over today, she'll be with ya till noon, then Josie will be here to keep ya company till I get home," I remind her, despite the fact she knows the routine well.

The way her chest sags shows how much she hates therapy

days but she's far too polite to admit it. Jimmer's tried a few different counselors since she's been here, and although what Samantha has done ain't exactly been groundbreaking, Everleigh seems comfortable with her, comfortable enough to be left alone so I'm guessing that means something.

I've barely finished my plate before it gets swiped from under me and taken to the basin. I shake my head and grin to myself when she quickly pours me a coffee and places it in front of me.

"You like Samantha, right?" I check, knowing that these sessions are important, I just wish they could make those night terrors go away, and stop her flinching if I get too close.

If Samantha's not helping, I'm sure we could find someone else.

"She's lovely." Everleigh starts cleaning up the mess I've made of the kitchen, which kinda defeats the whole point I was trying to make with this breakfast.

"Lovely? That all ya gotta say?" I take a sip of my coffee and narrow my eyes at her. I'll probably never know exactly what happened to her in that bunker she was kept in, but that doesn't mean that I don't think about it every day. Whether I'm with her or I ain't, these days I find it hard to concentrate on anything else.

"She's nice," Everleigh assures me, and when I drain the last of my coffee she takes the mug straight off me too.

"I gotta go, I'll be back home around six," I let her know, picking my hat up from the chair and placing it on my head. I wonder to myself how it might feel to reach over and kiss her the way Garrett does to Maisie when he leaves for work, then I curse myself for thinking that way. Everleigh is young. It's wrong of me to think of her like that, but I just can't help myself.

"Bye, Mitch." She follows me to the door, standing and

holding it open so she can watch me get in my truck. She always looks a little sad when I leave her, and I wonder if that's because she misses me when I'm gone. I like the idea of that a whole lot more than I should. I start up the engine and get confused when I see Josie's car bouncing across the terrain in the distance.

"See ya later," I call out the window as I pull away and drive toward Josie.

"How is she today?" she asks when we pull up beside each other. Josie's a bright girl and although this ain't part of her job description, she never complains. All the councelors who have dealt with Everleigh have said that she should have consistency. Maisie and Leia can't spare that kinda time with the little ones to look after and since Everleigh gets so nervous at the thought of meeting new people, we agreed to stick to the same person, Josie.

"She had another rough night but seems okay this mornin'. I thought you weren't gettin' here till lunchtime?" I question her.

"Samantha called and said she was running late. I know Everleigh panics if she's on her own for too long, I didn't want her locking herself in the bathroom again." She smiles sadly, reminding me of what happened last week when Josie got held up at an appointment. "I checked with Maisie and she can spare me, so here I am." This time, her smile is a little more joyful.

"I appreciate that, you have a good day." I nod my head before I leave her to it and make my way to the ranch.

Wade's still trying to break in the mare that Cole bought last week, while my bunkhouse boys, Tate and Finn, sit their lazy asses on the side of the corral and watch him fail.

"Ain't ya got work to be gettin' on with?" I call over to 'em and when Tate hears my voice and looks back over his shoulder, he quickly slides off the rail and heads toward me.

"We're just watchin' Wade waste his time," he tells me.

"Never let Cole loose at an auction again." Wade gets up from the floor and picks up his hat.

"She's impossible." He dusts it off before placing it back on his head.

"Ya ain't ready to give in already, are ya?" Cole looks smug as he rests his arms over the gate.

"What on earth made you part with hard-earned cash for this?" Wade questions his brother.

"His wife liked the color." Savannah slides her head under Cole's arm and wraps her arms around his waist. Things have been a lot less tense around here since they got their shit together and tied the knot.

That, and Wade's little boy being born really pulled the family together during a time of tragedy, I can't help wishing that Dalton was still here to be part of it.

For years I kept my nephew in the dark over who his father was. I was trying to protect him. I didn't want him to know that he wasn't wanted. In doing that, I denied him all those years he could have spent getting to know his brothers. I deeply regret that. All I can do now is be grateful that he had those few months of knowing who he really was and know how happy being accepted by his brothers made him.

"What the hell happened to you? I think I preferred you when you were a cold, callous bastard?" Wade glares at Cole as he jumps back on the saddle.

"It was you that told me how important it was to keep a pregnant woman happy." Cole strokes his hand proudly over the now, very prominent bump he's given his wife. One thing that can be said for a Carson man, is that they don't waste any time in the procreating department.

"Mitch," Garrett calls over as he steps off his porch. "Did ya see Josie on ya way here? She got a call sayin' Samantha couldn't make it." Garrett and the others may not have met Everleigh yet, but that don't mean they don't care. Everyone here has a general idea of what happened to her and they understand that it's gonna take some time to adjust.

When she's finally ready, Everleigh has got a whole bunch of decent people who wanna make her feel welcome, and that makes me real happy for her.

"Yeah, she explained and I appreciate ya sparin' her."

"Ain't a problem, I just wish she'd start makin' some steps forward, it can't be easy splittin' yourself between her and here."

"I don't mind at all." I nod, before making my way into the stable to saddle up JD.

"Mitch Hudson." I spin around when I hear my full name. " The woman at the guesthouse said you were the one to speak to about getting some employment around here." The young lad that stands in front of me is tall and has a good set of shoulders on him. He looks handy, even with his shiny boots and eyes that look far too kind to have seen any trouble.

"Name's Hunter and I'm looking for some work, sir." He holds out his hand and grips me firmly when I shake it.

"You know how to ride a horse, son?" I reach up and lift the brand-new Stetson off his head so I can examine it.

"No, sir, but I can learn."

"You know how to throw a rope?" I place it back on his head and flick the front of it up.

"No, but I pick up fast." He seems confident as well as determined, which is never a bad thing.

"You come lookin' for work on a ranch, and you can't ride a horse or rope a cow?" I laugh at him. "What am I supposed to hire ya for?"

The kid backs up a little, looking at the space around him, then taking the brand new gloves from outta his back pocket he slides 'em over his fingers.

"There's this." He heads over to the anvil on the far side of the stable and starts to lift it, without making no sound or breaking any sweat.

"It took both Finn and Tate to carry that in here after the blacksmith was done last week," I say my thoughts out loud as I stare at the boy in shock and realize he's still holding it.

"Well, I guess everyone's good for something," he tells me before placing it back down.

"You mean what ya say about being a fast learner?" I check, we got a lotta work coming up over the next few weeks and we could use the extra hands.

"Yes, sir, I was raised right, I wouldn't lie to ya." Something about those big, brown eyes steer me into believing him. There don't seem to be no malice in the boy, and he's proved that he's strong.

"Come on, I'll show ya to the bunkhouse." I tie JD back up and lead the boy back out to the yard.

"This here's Garrett," I introduce him to the boss. "Garrett, Hunter, he's as green as pea soup but he's strong," I assure him.

"Pleased to meet ya." Garrett holds out his hand.

"That guy there, who's failin' to get a hold on his filly, is Wade." I gesture my head into the corral. "And that love-struck thing over there is Cole," I point over to where he stands kissing Savannah. "They all own this place. It's them who pay your wages and me who ensures you earn 'em. You got that?"

"I got it." The boy nods his head as he takes it all in.

"Follow me." I lead him over to the bunkhouse.

Once inside I can see that it ain't being kept the way it should be, there are dishes piled up in the sink and empty bottles scattered all over from the night before.

"Excuse the mess." I lead the kid through the carnage, stopping when I get to Dalton's bunk. His bed is still made up, he's still got the poster of last June's Buckle Bunny of the Month pinned to his wall, and it hurts like hell to think he'll never sleep in here again.

"This one's free." I quickly move on, and stand beside the bunk in the corner. "You can get started straight away. First job ya got is to clean up this shit hole. We ain't got much time for teachin' so you'll have to learn quick, and I wanna hear stories about you practicin' your rope skills in your own free time. It's hard graft, it's shit pay, but there ain't a life better than it." I slap him on his big, burly shoulder before heading for the door.

"Mitch," he calls out before I can leave, and when I turn around the boy's wearing a huge grin on his face. "Thanks for taking a chance on me."

"Everyone gets one, not many get a second," I warn him before I leave to do some work.

The days are lonely and seem to go on forever when he's not here. I always try to busy myself around the cabin, hoping it will make the time go faster, but the place is so small and easy to keep clean, it takes no time at all.

Josie is kind and very thoughtful, but she stopped trying to make conversation with me a while ago when she realized it was never going anywhere. All her attempts just made us both feel uncomfortable, because as much as she, Mitch, and Samantha try to hide it, in reality I'm just a shell. I have no personality of my own anymore. I have no experience of this world that I've found myself in. And the only thing my sad existence has to look forward to, is him coming home to me.

I just see the pity on Josie's face whenever she walks through the door now. She spends most of the time she's here on the porch speaking to her friends on the phone but constantly checks on me with that same sad smile that tells me how grateful she is not to be me.

Times like this I wish I was better at the whole conversation thing. I'm confused by what happened this morning. Making breakfast is *my* job, and like all the chores I do around here, I do it to be useful and show my appreciation.

If Mitch starts to take that away from me I don't know what my purpose would be.

Every day I'm starting to feel a little stronger physically, the portion sizes of food I can manage get larger and I've already grown out of the clothes Jimmer sent me here with. The clothes Josie bought for me a few weeks ago fit much nicer and I feel better when I look in the mirror and see my hair growing back.

It's nowhere near as long as it used to be, but I can braid it now. Braiding it reminds me of Moma and how she used to be when Dad wasn't around. She'd hum to herself while she did mine and Addison's hair. It's a happy memory and one of very few I have with her. It also makes me think about Addison, my beautiful, big sister who I adored. The vision of her is clouded now, darkened by *his* sinister, cruel eyes. I remember how they used to come alive when he'd serve me one of her punishments.

"Everleigh?" Samantha, my therapist, lets herself in and I abandon the potatoes I'm peeling for dinner, moving to join her in the living area.

"I'm sorry I'm late. My little boy's sick, I had to arrange child care."

Josie knocks on the window from outside, waving at me with the phone still attached to her ear as she leaves. I nod gratefully, knowing that coming out here every day to babysit me must be a burden to her.

"How are you, Everleigh?" I focus my attention on Samantha when she asks, and take a seat on the couch beside her.

I take a breath and prepare myself for the attempts she'll make to claw inside my head and stir up all the misery inside it.

"Did you write anymore in that journal I gave you?" she asks.

I shake my head, knowing my answer will disappoint her. I don't want to go back there and let those thoughts loose. I don't want them to follow me here. This place is fresh and new. I'm safe here, and I know that because Mitch promised me. I'd much rather spend my evenings listening to him strum his guitar, or watching the way he cleans his rifles than write down my painful memories.

"That's fine. How about the letter your sister sent? Have you had the chance to read it?"

I shake my head at that too, feeling guilty for all the hatred I feel toward her. It's not how I want to feel, it's something that got planted inside me and was given all the resources to grow. If I could, I'd cut it out and love her the way I used to, but its roots are far too deep and I know that seeing her words on a piece of paper would be a trigger for me.

"That's okay, too. It's a goal we can work toward. It's very important that you have goals, Everleigh," she reminds me.

She's right of course, and each night I set my goal and I fail. All I want is just to get through a night without being dragged back into that bunker. But it doesn't matter how hard I try, he still manages to summon me in my sleep.

"I'll try and use the journal." I make her the same half-hearted promise that I made three days ago and hope she buys it.

"Okay." She seems to accept it, though I'm sure she's fully aware that I'm lying.

"Today I want to talk to you about—"

"Samantha, I'm really tired. I was up a lot last night. I think I should catch up on some sleep." I fake a yawn, relying on the fact that she constantly tells me how important it is that I make up for the lack of sleep I get at night.

"Everleigh, I know how hard this is, but we have to start somewhere. You can't heal if you won't talk about—"

"I don't want to talk about it because it feels like a disease, one that if I share will infest you too," I blurt out angrily. "I'm sorry. I didn't mean..."

Samantha nods her head back at me forgivingly.

"I promise that whatever you tell me, I can handle. I'm trained—"

"I wasn't. I had no *training* for what I went through. I thought that everything was right with the world I lived in, that you got chosen by your husband, and that you were taken care of by him. I thought I would be loved and that I'd have beautiful children." Samantha pulls that same sorry face that Josie greets me with every day and I realize that even trying to explain is hopeless.

"I'd like you to leave now." I stand up, trying my best to be assertive.

"Okay." I can see how disappointed she is, and I feel guilty for wasting her time but I can't deal with this today. Not while I'm worrying about what happened with Mitch this morning. "I can't force you to do anything. I wouldn't, even if I could. That's not how therapy works, but I can tell you that the only way to get better is to let those memories and those thoughts free from your mind. Speak to someone, write them down, head outside, and scream it out to the mountains, but don't keep it inside. If you do, you're only letting that disease eat away at you." She smiles as she picks up her bag, heads for the door, and leaves.

I stare around the empty cabin as I hear her car pull away, and instead of messaging Josie and asking her to come back, I decide to brave being alone.

I look at the chair that Mitch sits in to eat the meals I cook for him and smile fondly when I think of the enjoyment he gets from eating them. It's a really good feeling making someone happy and I wish there was more I could do for him. He never talks about it, but I'm fully aware that his life has changed because of me. He used to live on the ranch with all the other cowboys that work for the Carsons, no doubt it was much more fun there than it is here. Me being here, and relying on that promise he made me the night I came, has confined him to this cabin with just me and my nightmares.

Something happened between us the night his nephew died, he came home sad and covered in blood, and right from the second he walked through the door, I could see he needed somebody. The strong, sometimes grumpy, man that I'd come to know looked vulnerable. Maybe that's why when he touched his hand to my cheek I didn't flinch away. I allowed his fingertips to linger on my skin and ever since, I've thought about letting them do it again. Sometimes, when I wake from one of my dreams, I imagine being wrapped up in those big, strong arms of his. They look as if they could hold off the whole world.

He hasn't attempted to touch me again and I know why. During my first few weeks here he looked so hurt when I flinched at him. Maybe if he knew what I'd been through he'd understand, but I'm too ashamed to tell him, and something tells me that despite me being an inconvenience, he cares for me. He wouldn't want to hear the horrors of my past any more than I'd want to tell them.

I last two hours before I feel the walls closing in on me and even picking up a book and turning on the television doesn't prevent me from thinking about the long, torturous hours that I'd spend staring into the black. The phone is right there on the table. I could easily call Josie. I know how to use the phone now. I could even text her, but I decide to push through and try to be brave. Having Josie here as my babysitter can't go on forever, and as sad as it makes me to admit, Mitch can't either.

It's past six when Mitch steps through the door. He's looking worn out and is covered in dirt, but it feels a little bit easier to breathe now he's home.

"Evenin', darlin'." He smiles at me as he hangs up his hat and heads straight for the refrigerator.

I keep stirring the soup I made for us and try to ignore the tiny butterflies he puts in my stomach every time he comes near. I've never felt anything like it before and I know it can't be nerves because nothing about this man scares me. In fact, I find everything about Mitch fascinating. Like the way his beard has grey streaks that match his hair, and the way his dark eyes watch me sometimes. I love the way he sings in the shower and how his fingers look when they play his guitar. But most of all, I like how safe I feel when I'm around him.

The night he brought me here, he told me he'd never let anyone hurt me, and the look he had on his face and the tone of his voice made me believe him. Mitch isn't perfect, I sense a darkness inside him and I know that, just like the Soul men, he would take a life if he had to. That's what makes me so confident in his word.

"How did things go with Samantha?" he asks me as he washes the dirt off his hands and scrubs his face over in the basin.

"The usual." I shrug, knowing that he'd like to report better back to Jimmer.

"And what do we have tonight?" He keeps his distance as he looks over my shoulder.

"It's some kind of soup, I got the recipe from one of the cookbooks the girls sent with Josie." I smile back at him. I've never met the girls who live on the ranch, but they show me kindness. When I first arrived they sent me clothes through Josie and an open invitation to visit them whenever I feel up to it. When I mentioned to Josie that I felt bad for cooking Mitch my same recipes, she must have mentioned it to them because she came back the next day with this book.

"Smells good." I turn to look over my shoulder, not realizing how close he is, and when we bump noses I drop the spoon in my hand and spill hot soup all over my dress.

"Shit! I'm sorry." Mitch steps back, while I waft the fabric that's burning my skin, trying to cool it off. He rushes to the basin and grabs a cloth, soaking it with water, and I freeze when he goes to grab my dress. His hand wraps around my waist to steady me as he wipes the front of it with the damp cloth and I feel every beat my heart makes as his strokes ease the burn.

He's acted on impulse and when he realizes, his strokes slow right down and his eyes look up at me.

"I'm sorry." He quickly releases me, taking a step back and holding out the cloth for me to take. "I... just..."

"Thank you." I take it from him and wipe myself over. "I should chang—"

"Yeah, you do that and I'll clean up here." He looks down at the spoon and the splattered soup that's all over the floor. All of a sudden things feel really awkward between us. Why am I so surprised that him holding me like that felt exactly like I imagined it would? And why am I so desperate for him to do it again?

I smile at him before I scurry off to change my dress.

CHAPTER 3

MITCH

I fucked up, I heard her yell in pain and I went into autopilot to fix the problem. I forgot the rules, I touched her and now she's freaking out. We may not have made a lot of progress over the past few months, but there've been little things that have made all the difference. She talks, not all that much, but enough. She smiles, and I've been getting the feeling just lately that she's content with her life here.

I swear, the other day I heard her humming while she was changing the sheets on her bed.

I know how fragile she is, that anything around her could be a trigger, and what I just let happen could have set her right back.

She comes back out the bedroom in a pair of jeans and a tee, looking at me awkwardly through her lashes as she steps back in front of the stove.

"Look, Ev. I didn't mean to—"

"It's fine, you were helping me." She smiles.

"Yeah, but I forgot and I'm so—"

"Please, don't apologize, you were being kind. *I'm okay,*" she assures me with a soft whisper that I want so desperately to believe.

We eat our dinner in silence, and as I watch her sip her soup from her spoon, I can't help wondering what's going on in her head.

She's clearly trying to be brave, and the thought of her not feeling safe here anymore is making me nervous.

"That was great." I lift up both our bowls, taking them to the basin when we're finished, and she quickly gets up from her chair and comes after me.

"No, I'll clean these. You rest." She snatches them off me frantically.

"I got it, darlin', why don't ya see if there's anythin' decent on?" I nod my head toward the TV in the corner.

"Please, you need to let me do it." She keeps a firm grip on the dishes, shocking me with her determination. Up until now, all I've seen from this girl is meekness.

"Everleigh, we have to—"

"Why are you doing this? Breakfast this morning, now the dishes? It's *my* job. I have to—"

"Sweetheart," I remind myself not to touch her when my hand automatically reaches out, it felt too good for those few seconds when I did it before and I hate having to retract it. "It's not your job, and I ain't tryin' to do anythin' to upset ya. I'm just helpin' out. I wanted you to settle in right when you first came here. I was doin' things your way, but it's been six months now, ya gotta start comin' around to another way of thinkin'." I shake my head, tryin' to explain it to her. "Around here, men value their women, they ain't just cooks and dishwashers." I smile at her as she stares up at me confused.

"But if I don't do these things I don't have a purpose, I'm just a burden to you." Her pretty, blue eyes fill with tears and when one releases, I decide to test her boundaries. The night Dalton died she let me touch her, we never spoke about it after so she won't have any idea how much it meant to me. Right now, I want to show her that she has a far greater purpose than she could ever know. Everleigh holds on to her breath when I slowly raise my thumb and gently stroke that tear away.

"You're no burden, Everleigh, and you *have* got a purpose. You make this old man very happy to come home every night, and don't you forget it." My voice comes out deep and groggy, I guess it's because she makes me nervous. I feel such a strong pressure to get things right around her.

Her lips raise into a shy, little smile as if she likes the sound of what I just said.

"Well, how about you wash and I'll dry?" she suggests.

"That sounds a helluva lot like a compromise." I laugh as I toss her a dishtowel and roll up my sleeves.

I sit in my chair and pretend to be interested in what's on the TV. I love that even after all this time, Everleigh still stares at the thing as if it's some kinda magical portal. Jimmer was right, here is a good place for her to get a taste of what the real world is like without being overwhelmed by it. Having the TV has helped her get a glimpse of what's beyond the cabin walls and she's always fascinated by whatever's on it.

"You like this show?" I ask, attempting to make conversation with her. The silences are never awkward, but tonight I swear I felt something shift between us. I've touched her twice and neither time did she flinch. It feels as if her barrier is coming down.

"I like it all, it's amazing. Yesterday I watched a documentary on mountain goats." She smiles so brightly, that for just a second it would be easy to forget that she's been through hell.

"Mountain goats." I chuckle to myself. "You know you got a

whole bunch of wildlife right outside your front door? We're borderin' Yellowstone National Park."

She bites her lip nervously as she looks toward the wooden door she uses as her shield. Since she's been here she's barely stepped out onto the porch, and I know it's because she's scared of the great unknown she thinks is out there.

"Just the other day, me and Tate saw a golden eagle."

"A golden eagle?" She moves to the edge of the couch, intrigued by what I've told her.

"Yep, you get all kindsa birds around here. Maybe one day we could take a ride and I'll show ya?"

"On your horse?" She frowns.

"It's the best way, no engine to scare anythin' away. I promise there ain't no feelin' like takin' a ride on a sunny day."

"I've never ridden a horse before." She shakes her head, looking embarrassed.

"Well, I think that's somethin' we oughtta change."

"Like you doing the dishes." The smile on her face is different to before, it's got a hint of mischief behind it that gets an instant reaction outta my dick.

"Like me doin' the dishes." I shake my head and sit back in my chair.

———

"What ya doin' to that poor boy?" I question Tate and Finn when I see Hunter getting tossed off his saddle by Buck.

"Just havin' a little fun, you said yaself it's best for him to get thrown in at the deep end."

"Hey now, whoooa now." I step into the corral and take Buck's reins. Holding him steady and giving Hunter a chance to get his breath back.

"Ya good?" I check, watching him readjust himself on the saddle.

Buck's a good horse, but he's got personality. You gotta have a whole lotta confidence for him to respect you.

"I'm great, boss, just learning the ropes." Hunter leans forward, tapping Buck's neck enthusiastically, and when he throws his front legs up in the air, the boy clings around his neck for dear life.

"Get off the saddle." I shake my head then scowl across at Finn and Tate, who are still looking amused with themselves. "Ain't you pair got work to be gettin' on with?" I scold 'em before leading Buck back to the stable.

"Pay 'em no mind, they were just havin' some fun with ya," I tell the kid as he follows me inside.

"It's fine, boss, I get it. I'm new." Hunter looks a little embarrassed but still determined. "I'll get the hang of it, sir, I promise."

"They teach ya how to saddle up?" I ask.

"Yeah, I can do that," he assures me.

"Saddle up that stallion over there." I nod my head over to the other side of the stable. "He's calm, he's gentle, he's perfect to learn on."

"On it, boss." Hunter gets straight to work while I grab my tack and start saddling up JD.

I keep my eye on the boy for the best part of the day, he wasn't lying when he said he can pick things up quickly, it's barely past noon before he looks competent on the saddle.

I try not to be distracted by what happened last night, and how good it felt after all this time to touch Everleigh. There was definitely something between us, something I shouldn't contemplate because it can't be real. I can't get wrapped up in whatever that something might be. This girl knows no better, her only experiences come from the life she had back in that village. One day soon she's gonna find herself. She's gonna wanna move on and see what the world has to offer her. I made it this far in my life with my heart still intact, I ain't about to let it break now.

CHAPTER 4

EVERLEIGH

I hear my mom crying before the door to my room swings open with force.

"You're needed, girl." The elder who steps into my room, grabs me and drags me from my bed. It's cold and all I have covering my body is my cotton nightgown. I have nothing on my feet, but he doesn't seem to care as he shoves me out the front door, causing me to fall onto the gravel outside.

"Abraham is waiting for you in the chapel," my father tells me, keeping his head low. He's refusing to make eye contact with me or my mother, who is beating his arm with her fists and begging him to make them stop.

"Control your woman, Thomas." The elder lifts me off the ground by my armpits and then pushes me in the back to force me forward. It leaves me no choice but to head toward the chapel that's built in the center of our village.

Two men stand either side of the doors, both holding lit torches, and as I pass them I shudder because I know whatever waits for me inside can't be good. Earlier today, our leader killed my sister's friend in front of the entire village. I wept for him, maybe that's why I'm here. I step through the door and when I look up to the altar I see our great leader, my sister's husband, *laid out flat on the platform. He's so still and pale that I wonder if he's dead.*

"Step closer, child," he calls out to me, proving that he's alive. With dread leaking into my stomach I do as he commands.

My palms are sweating and my heart is beating out of my chest because I know what's coming. It's not unheard of for God to command a man to take one of his wives' sisters as his own. Abraham may already have three wives but as our leader, he is the man above all men. God speaks directly to him, and I'm here because he's chosen me.

"Your sister escaped me tonight," he croaks, and a lump wedges in my throat and nearly chokes me when I take in what he says. It's a shock, but at the same time, I have to try not to show how happy it makes me. All her life, Addison has wondered what life is like beyond the village. I guess she's finding out. I must pray that she remains pure of its temptations.

"She ran, but not before she tried to kill me." I can see how angry he is and suddenly his reason for lying down is clear. Addison did this to him.

"I hope you are okay, sir," I lie, as I stand beside him and imagine how scared Addison must've been to strike. She may have been curious of it, but she knows life beyond the gates is dangerous. She must have faced some horrors if she believed it was a better option than here.

"I shall recover, but your sister's sins must be punished," he tells me, clutching his side as he speaks.

"Please don't hurt her." I drop to my knees and beg him. Elders are the only ones who ever leave the village, the thought of them out there hunting her down makes me sick with worry.

"She won't be harmed, not while I have you." He smiles as he takes my wrist in his cold, wrinkly hand and holds me firm.

"You shall be her replacement, you shall replenish her sins in her absence and you will serve me," he explains, making the

terror inside me spread through my veins and turn my blood cold.

Rough arms grip me from behind and start dragging me away. I try to scream but fear clasps around my throat and cuts off any noise.

"I'll be seeing you, Everleigh," Abraham promises.

The cold bites my skin as the two men carry me across the village, one of them holding his hand over my mouth so I can't scream for help. I fight and thrash against them, trying desperately to get away. Maybe I could escape too. The world outside may be unknown and frightening, but it has to be better than this. Now I know why Father couldn't look at me, he's an elder too, he knew what was happening tonight and he wasn't prepared to fight for me.

I see Abraham's son, Solomon, standing by their house holding a lantern. When I see that the doors that lead down into the bunker are open beside him, I fight even harder to get free.

Solomon has always given me the creeps. I caught him cutting open a pretty, white bird once, while it was still alive. He had it pinned by its wings and I saw the pleasure he had on his face as he slowly sliced through its feathers to open up its guts.

Sometimes I've noticed him look at me the same way as he did that bird, and it makes my stomach roll.

"I'll take it from here." He snatches my arm and starts dragging me down the stairs, and when the lantern lights up the cold, damp walls I swear I see splatters of blood on them. There's only dirt for ground down here and when he places me in the corner, I slump weakly onto the floor when my legs give in.

"Your sister made a mistake tonight, little dove," Solomon slides his fingers through my hair and makes me shudder. Moma always told me it would probably be him who I'm given to and the thought has always made me sick. "Your sister fucked it up *for us both. You were gonna be mine, Everleigh, and I was gonna treat you good," he whispers.*

"Please, Solomon," I beg him, praying that if he does care about me he might fix this.

"It's too late now, little dove. You belong to him. I just hope you survive it." He kisses my forehead before clamping two heavy shackles around my wrists and leaving me in the dark

I slam my journal closed and clutch it to my chest. My pulse is beating far too fast as those memories swirl around in my head like a tornado dragging me into its center.

"You okay?" Josie looks up from the magazine she's reading.

"I'm fine, just a little, ummm..." I can't put into words what's going through my mind. Digging up old bones has made me feel as if I was there again, living it all over, and yet at the same time, I've freed up some space in my head by getting the words out.

"Is that the journal Samantha gave you?" Josie gets up from the couch and moves toward me, and I clutch it close to me to guard it.

"Yeah." I nod.

"I think it's good that you're using it." She sits beside me and gives me that sad smile again. "Can I be honest with you?" Her head tips sideways as she lets out a deep breath.

"I'd like that." I smile back at her.

"I never know how to be around you, or what to say. I know a little about what you've been through, but not the whole story. I feel as if me, just acting normal around you after all you've suffered, is insensitive."

"Thank you." I smile at her.

"For what? Being awkward and useless?" Josie laughs.

"For being truthful, and for coming here almost every day

to keep me company despite not knowing how to act. I've never once thought you were insensitive," I assure her.

"You wanna know another secret?" She leans in closer. "This place is much more peaceful than the ranch. I don't mind at all." She winks at me, before getting up and heading back to the couch.

Josie leaves a little before Mitch is due to get home. Each day when he walks through the door, those butterflies that stir in my stomach seem to get stronger. After the way his arm wrapped around my body, and his rough hand so tenderly stroked my cheek yesterday, I've been obsessing over him doing it again.

"Good day?" he asks, hanging up his hat the same way he always does.

"Yeah, me and Josie ended up making a casserole— What happened to your hand?" I freeze when I see the bandage wrapped around his palm and the blood soaking through it.

"It ain't nothin', just tore it open on a loose nail. I'll get it washed up and pour some alcohol on it." He shrugs like it's no big deal but I quickly fetch a bowl, filling it with warm water, before I place it on the table.

"Sit down." I look around the kitchen, knowing for sure that there's a first aid box here somewhere. I put it away myself when I reorganized the cupboards last month.

"You don't need to make no fuss." He shakes his head as I reach up on my toes into the cabinet above the refrigerator and locate it.

I wait for him to sit down before I take the seat beside him and unwind the bandage from his palm. The cut looks nasty but not deep enough for stitches. Taking his wrist, I gently lower his hand into the warm water so it can soak. I don't look up at him but I can feel his eyes studying me the way they always do. I often wonder what he's thinking when he does that. It's intense and a little overbearing but I like it all the same. I like that this man takes an interest in me. I like what he said to me last night about how he feels coming home, and I like that it's always his voice that guides me out of my nightmares.

"That's feelin' better already." He smiles at me when I lift his hand out and gently pat it dry with a towel. I stroke over the uninjured part of his palm with my finger, appreciating his rough, overworked skin, and when I'm brave enough to look up at him he's frowning at me in confusion.

"You good?" he checks.

"You have hard-working hands." I smile at him. Abraham and Solomon's hands were so smooth, and always felt so slimy on my skin. I imagine it would feel very different to be touched by hands like these.

"They've seen their fair share of work over the years." He laughs, then flinches when I dab the open wound with alcohol. I make sure it's clean before taking a fresh gauze and rewrapping it with a new bandage.

"There." I smile proudly. It's nice to feel like I've helped him, after all he does for me.

My hand lingers over his for longer than it should, maybe it's because I enjoy the warmth of his skin, or because I'm proud of myself for pushing my boundaries. But there's a niggle inside me that tells me it's something different. Something that makes me want to cry again just so I can have him wipe away my tears.

"Thank you," he tells me in that low, husky voice. His injured hand lifts up and strokes my cheek, pushing back my hair as his fingertips brush over my skin like he can sense it's what I need.

He looks nervous and unsure, so I rest my head a little into his palm to let him know it's okay.

A loud thud interrupts the moment and Mitch suddenly pulls back. It's followed by another loud bang and I stand up, staring at the door, trying to control the panic I can feel taking over all my senses.

"Relax, it's okay. I got it," Mitch tries to assure me as he makes his way to the door and opens it.

"Finn, I thought I told ya not to—"

"Garrett's called a meetin', we tried to call but your phone's off." Whoever is on the other side of the door interrupts him with an urgent voice.

"I... ummm... I..." Mitch looks between me and the door with that unsure expression on his face again.

"Can someone get hold of Josie?" he asks.

"I'll be fine," I cut in, smiling at him bravely. "I have to start getting used to being on my own." I shrug, trusting in the words that he promised me. I'm safe here.

"Ya sure?" Mitch opens the door a little wider and when I see the young man on the other side of it, he lifts his hat to me politely and smiles.

"You must be Everleigh. Name's Finn." He introduces himself and holds out his hand, quickly retracting it after Mitch subtly shakes his head.

"Pleased to meet you." I manage a smile for him. Trusting that he's not a threat. Mitch wouldn't allow him to be here if he was.

"You never told us she was so pretty." He looks back to Mitch, who grabs his hat and quickly shoos him out the door.

"I'll be back as soon as I can." He turns back to face me,

moving closer to assure me. "You can bolt the door after I've left."

"Okay, stay safe." I smile, and when he looks down between us and sees that I've gripped hold of his hand, he smiles too. I don't know much about what happens on the other side of the cabin door but I get the sense Mitch lives among danger. I'd hate for anything to happen to him.

"See ya soon." He backs away and leaves.

I move toward the window, watching him get into the guy's truck before they speed away.

CHAPTER 5

MITCH

"**W**hat the fuck is that?" I stare at the severed head that's resting on the porch at the long camp.

"That's a—"

"I know what it fuckin' is! I *mean* what's it doin' here?" I interrupt Noah. Fuckin' River Boys always got something smart to say.

"*This* was sent by courier to the Carson Ranch and addressed to 'The Mayor'." Tate scratches the back of his neck as we all stare at the decomposing face that's looking up at us

"Well, do any of ya know whose body it belongs to?" I look around at all the dumbstruck faces, wondering where the hell Garrett and his brothers are.

"I'm tellin' ya, that's Bucky Hall." Sawyer lights himself a smoke as he takes a seat on a log beside the fire.

"Bucky Hall, didn't he die years ago?" I swear I ain't seen that old man in over a decade.

"Nah, he's just been a recluse. My gran would have me go check in on him from time to time, but I stopped last year after he pulled a rifle on me," Sawyer explains.

"He pulled a rifle on ya?" Zayne laughs.

"Guess the old boy didn't wanna be bothered." Sawyer

shrugs, and when I get a sniff at what he's smokin' and realize it ain't just tobacco, I snatch it from his hand.

"You don't need that shit, not now." I stub it out on the rafter. I respect the River Boys. On a good day, I even like the fuckers, but they still have a lot to learn.

For decades, the Carsons have branded the men who are loyal to them, men who will do whatever it takes to ensure our town is protected. Noah, Sawyer, and Zane may not be cowboys like the men who were branded before them, but they've all earned the mark they've got on their chests.

I'm without doubt that they have an agenda of their own, Noah Wylde has connections that go far beyond our quaint little town, but they're a handy trio to have onboard and they've proved their loyalty time and time again.

We all look out toward the track when we hear the truck speeding toward us. Garrett skids to a stop before he gets out, slams his door, and marches toward us with a murderous look on his face.

"We all know who fuckin' did this." He kicks the head across the porch like it's a soccer ball, outta frustration.

"Garrett, you can't lose your head," Wade tells him once he's gotten out the passenger seat.

"Don't you think that's in poor taste?" Noah sniggers, his eyes flicking down to the head, and we all look shocked when Garrett grabs him by the shirt and pins him to the cabin wall.

"You think this is funny? My wife opened that fuckin' package." I can see the rage in his eyes, how his hands tremble, and I know from past experience that there ain't no limits to his anger.

"Garrett." I step in before things get outta hand, I also keep my eyes on Cole as he paces the steps in front of him. Hell knows *what's* going through his mind.

"Who do ya think it is?" I slowly ease Garrett down and

give Noah a warning look over my shoulder. He straightens himself out and smirks as he backs down.

"Ain't it obvious? Things have been quiet around here, now Mason's sister has moved her family into that ranch, we get this. I swear she knows what we did to her brother and nephews."

"She can only speculate, there ain't no evidence." Wade shakes his head.

"Well, speculation is clearly enough for her. Bucky Hall was refusin' to move from his homestead, his land is smack bang in the middle of the plans for that new freeway the council is trying to get passed. If they get permission that land value is gonna skyrocket. Stubborn old bastard wasn't ever gonna let a road be built through his home and I can assure you all, he would never sell to a Mason. He told me that himself." Garrett stares at what's left of him with a hint of sadness in his eyes. "She did this, she killed him so she could purchase his land, and she sent that as a warnin' to us." He points to the head.

"Well, if that's the case, she's an idiot. You're the fuckin' mayor now," Noah reminds him, and I can see by the look on Garrett's face that he didn't want a reminder of that fact.

Garrett Carson ain't the kind of man who likes attention, he's a simple man, a hard worker who ain't afraid to do what's necessary. Harvey Marston turned all that around when he showed up in town a few months ago and started making his demands. His organization needed someone like Garrett to be in control and although my boss ain't one who usually takes orders, he will do anything for the town he raises his family in. If Garrett hadn't taken the seat, Harvey would have found someone who would, and it's better the devil you know than the devil you don't.

"That ain't gonna make a difference. That woman has vengeance in mind. I saw that in the sadistic smile she gave me in chapel last week."

"Come on, Garrett, she was just introducin' herself." Wade tries to play it down.

"She knows we killed her brother and nephews and she's out for blood." Garrett grips the porch rail with both hands and lowers his head between them.

"So what do we do about it?" I ask, trying to keep him focused.

"We do nothin', not until I've sussed her out. She's only been in town a few weeks, she's already kicked her own nephew outta his home. So we know she's ruthless and ruthless people usually end up makin' mistakes." He turns his head back to look at me, and I can tell by the look on his face that he's back in control. "Tate and Finn, I need you to go speak to Joe Mason, find out everythin' you can about his aunt, anythin' he can tell us could be useful." He sends them off.

"Wait, didn't Joe inherit the ranch?" Sawyer looks surprised.

"Nope, his daddy cut him outta the will because he's a homophobic cunt." Garrett lights himself a smoke and takes a long, deep breath. "Not that Joe cares, he didn't want the place anyway. Him and Dexter got themselves a homestead on the border of town which suits him nicely. I'll bet he's about as happy to see his aunt show up as we are."

"Noah, I need you and your boys to get rid of that." Garrett points his cigarette toward the head, before taking a seat on the porch step and massaging his temple.

"You wanna tell me what's up?" I take a seat next to him, sensing that something's off, other than the severed head. Garrett's had far more than this to contend with in the past and he's not let it get to him.

"She shouldn't have had to see that." He shakes his head.

"No, she shouldn'a but she did, and you'll be there for her. That girl of yours is made of strong stuff."

"I just feel like I'm on a treadmill, one problem gets fixed then another one shows up."

"Ain't that the Carson way?" I smack him on the back, and just as I'm about to rise to my feet, I hear a horse come up behind me and I quickly spin around.

"Hunter, what ya doin' out here?" I ask, suddenly very aware of the fact Noah has Bucky Hall's head on full display

"You told me to practice, me and Blaze must have done eight miles and som—" The kid's face turns gray when he sees the head swingin' by its hair in Noah's fist, and then he starts to gag.

"What's up? Ain't ya ever seen a rottin' head before?" Noah tosses it at him and when his hands automatically reach out to catch it, he throws it in the air in disgust and falls off his saddle. Zayne and Sawyer chuckle and although Cole and Garrett remain serious, I notice Wade trying hard not to laugh with 'em.

"This ain't a fuckin' joke." Cole turns around and narrows his eyes. "Bucky Hall was a good man, you show him some respect." His head turns to Hunter who's now on his feet, hunched over and gagging by his horse's back legs.

"You're new round here, ain't ya?" Garrett steps closer to him and as Hunter stands up straight and wipes his mouth with the back of his hand, I see the fear in his eyes.

"You wanna take a ride again and head in the other direction, what goes on at this line camp is the business of branded men. And what ya saw here today..." Garrett crouches down and picks Bucky's head up from the floor, dusting off the top of his gray hair. "You forget about." He passes it back to Noah. "Ya understand me, boy?"

"Yes, sir." Hunter nods and when he attempts to get back on his saddle, his foot slips from the stirrup. The color quickly returns to his cheeks, flaming red as he makes his second attempt, this time managing to lift himself up, Then Cole slaps Blaze on his ass to send him on his way.

"You think he needs a firmer warnin'?" Cole cracks his knuckles as he watches him ride off.

"Nah, you saw how scared he was, ain't no way he's talkin'." Wade shakes his head.

"I gotta get back to Maisie, she was pretty shook up." Garrett nods for his brothers to follow him back to his truck. "Come on, we'll give ya a lift back to your cabin on the way." He smiles at me sadly.

I smile as we pull up to the cabin, and I see the oil lamp on the porch has been lit. Everleigh started doing that about two months ago, and I never would have thought such a simple gesture could bring with it so much appreciation.

"How is the girl?" Garrett asks, gripping the wheel and still looking tense.

"She's okay, still don't say much, and refuses to leave the cabin. I don't think the shrink she's talkin' to is doin' much good."

"You know, if it's a burden I can make other arrangements just because Jimmer's d—"

"She ain't a burden, and she's fine where she is," I snap at him as he pulls to a stop outside the cabin. The thought of her being anywhere but here doesn't just make me mad, it makes me fuckin' hurt.

"I think you're goin' soft, old man." Cole leans forward and kneads both my shoulders.

"And you're a fine one to talk," I remind him. There was a time when I thought Cole was lost to the darkness, but that sassy girl from L.A. dragged him right back out of it.

"You like her, don't ya?" Of course, Wade has to stick his two cents worth in too.

"I like her just fine. Same way I like all you assholes. Everleigh is a nice girl and she didn't deserve what happened to her, but she's half my age." My own words wound me as I get outta the truck and slam the door.

Stepping up onto the porch, I turn off the lantern and knock on the door.

"Everleigh, it's me."

I hear the bolts on the other side of the door move and when she opens it I like how she looks pleased to see me.

"You okay?" I check.

"I am now." She smiles as she steps away from the door and gets back to the couch, picking up the book she must have read four times over, and she begins to read.

S olomon plunges the sponge into the bucket of cold water and wrings it out before slapping it against my skin. I stand, shivering, with my back to the wall and my dignity in tatters. I hate that he won't release me from my shackles so I can do this myself. I hate the way he takes his time lifting up my nightdress and hooking it behind my head, and I hate the way his eyes linger on my body as his tongue slides out of his mouth to wet his lips.

"He's getting stronger every day. Soon he will visit you," he tells me as he slowly massages the sponge over my skin. His motions are so precise and focused I can tell he's enjoying my humiliation. I hold my breath as he squeezes the sponge and makes the water trickle over my breast.

"You have such a beautiful body, Everleigh, it's so sad that he wants to ruin it."

I gasp when he leans down, taking one of my nipples in his mouth and sucking it harshly.

"Please, Solomon," I beg, I have no idea how long I've been in here but even the luxury of being clean isn't worth this.

"It was supposed to be mine, there's no harm in me sampling it." He smiles up at me as he rolls his tongue around my nipple, and I try so hard to hold my tears in it feels as if my cheeks will shatter.

Everything about this is so confusing. Solomon touches me in all the ways I hate, and yet he shows me such kindness. He comes down here to wash me every few days, and just yesterday he snuck me down some fresh bread so I didn't just have what the elders provide for me.

"We could still be together, we could run away. Just us." I use whatever tactic I can to get me out of what's coming. The whole village saw what Abraham did to Charlie, he slit his throat in front of everyone when he found out he was bringing in medication from beyond the gates to help his brother. I can't imagine what he has planned for me.

"You have the devil of your sister in you." Solomon laughs at me as he soaks the sponge and shoves it between my legs, rubbing me as if he's trying to draw something out of me. "Should have been mine, and now it will be wasted," he snarls as he continues to assault me, and I quickly put all my efforts into blanking him out.

I try to think of better things like Addison being free, and how it used to feel sneaking into her bed to make up stories late at night when she still lived at home.

"You know some women take pleasure in their men," Solomon grunts as he takes out his manhood and lets it press against my stomach.

I don't believe that's true, I don't think anyone could take pleasure in the way he touches me. He slides his body against mine, thrusting his cock between us and making me squirm.

"I think you'd have liked it to be me who made you a woman, Everleigh." I'm shocked when he takes himself in his hand and starts beating it through his fist roughly. Then his breaths get heavier as his lips press over mine and his tongue invades my mouth.

I can't push him away because my hands are shackled, and so my only choice is to remain still and hope for it to be over. My tears come, along with the retching of my stomach and I say a silent prayer for it to stop.

"Say my name, Everleigh, I wanna hear it." He continues to tug himself through his fist, his face distorting like he's in some kind of pain. "Say my name like it should have been spoken on our wedding night," he growls desperately.

"Solomon." I do as I'm told, hoping it'll make him stop, and when he drops the sponge from his other hand he uses it to grip my shoulder.

His body stiffens as his cock erupts, coating my skin with something warm and sticky as his fingers indent my flesh. He breathes through his nostrils intensely as he watches his mess slip over my skin, then he smiles at me with satisfaction as he reaches over my head and pulls the nightgown back over my body.

"Our secret, little dove." He presses his finger over my lips before he leaves, taking the bowl and sponge with him.

I close the journal and place it in the drawer of my nightstand when I can't stand to think about it anymore. I've barely gotten started on the horrors that happened to me, and reliving it in my head is hard, but if this is the path to healing then I'll suffer each step to get to the end. My mouth is dry, and I swear I can taste him on my lips now. So getting out of bed, I pull on a robe and head to the kitchen for some water.

The air is hot and sticky, and the fact I'm already sweating doesn't help. When I open the door and step into the living area, I expect to find Mitch asleep on the couch. I *do not* expect him to only be wearing his boxers.

The blanket that should be covering him is in a ball on the floor, and I take the time to admire him while he sleeps.

I've never seen a man without his clothes on before. And, although I can tell from the shirts he wears that Mitch is built well, they do not do him justice.

His shoulders and arms are muscular and strong, evidence, like his rough hands, that he works hard. I step closer and tilt my head as I examine the light dusting of gray hair that covers his chest and how it trails down to his torso, which is just as taut and solid as the rest of him.

The black boxers he wears are tight, and when I see what they're concealing bulging from under them, I quickly focus my eyes back up his body. There's a scar, or something like it on the left side of his chest, and I wonder how he got it as I watch it rise and fall steadily.

He looks so peaceful. It must feel good to sleep without being haunted by your past. It's been so long since I was taken to that bunker I can't remember what good dreams are like.

What I do remember is how nice it felt to touch him earlier, how all my fears are gradually starting to fade away when I'm with him. I want to feel that warmth again. I want to touch him and feel his heart beating under that chest.

Slowly, without my full permission, my fingers reach out, trembling as they slide through the hair on his chest and stroke over the letters that are scarred into his skin.

"What the fuck?" He snaps awake and grabs my wrist tight. Sitting up, and searching around the room for any threat, before looking at me in confusion.

"Everleigh?" He's still clutching at my wrist while he regulates his breathing.

"You okay? Ya hear somethin'?" I shake my head back at him, trying to find a reasonable explanation in my head as to why I would be here touching him while he sleeps.

"You scared me." He laughs to himself, then looking down he realizes that he's still got a grip on me and quickly releases. "Shit, I'm sorry, did I hurt ya?"

"No," I whisper, feeling my cheeks get warmer and my pulse rise.

"You have another bad dream?" he checks with that sweet concern in his dark brown eyes.

"No, I'm fine. I was just... I... I saw the blanket on the floor, I was going to cover you back over." I smile helplessly. It's not a complete lie, the thought had crossed my mind before I got distracted.

"That's sweet of ya, darlin', but it's hot as balls in here." He looks back down between our bodies and when I realize that my hand is still resting on his chest, I swallow thickly. I can feel his heart beating fast and when I lift my eyes back up to his and he smiles, my own heart picks up to match his rhythm.

"Water." The word blurts out from nowhere. He frowns and I stand up to try and get a hold of myself. "I came out here for water and I... Do you want some water?" I ask him, hearing the nerves in my voice. I can't believe I let curiosity get the better of me, and even worse, I got caught out.

"Water would be great, but you sit down. I'll get it." He moves past me and heads toward the kitchen while I slide my hands through my hair and try to steady my breathing.

"So, you havin' trouble sleepin'?" He hands me a glass of water with ice, before taking a seat on the couch beside me. We've never sat this close before, our shoulders are almost touching and the fact that he has nothing on from the waist up makes it feel even stranger.

"A little. I'm sorry I woke you." I take a sip before reaching forward to place it on the coffee table.

"Nah, you're alright." He settles his glass down next to mine and rests back.

"You wanna talk about whatever it is? I ain't no shrink but I've been told I'm a good listener."

"Trust me, you don't want to hear it, and I sure don't want to tell you it." I smile sadly because just the thought of explaining to Mitch what I endured back at the village makes me burn in shame. I may not know much about the real world, but the more time I spend in it, the more I realize how crazy that place was. It makes me question how we were all so convinced that such an evil man could lead us on the right path.

"Well, if you change your mind, I'll always be here."

"Always?" I check, wondering how long I can expect this man to put his life on hold for me.

"For as long as you need me." His hand slides over to cover the one I have resting on my knee and I don't flinch. In fact, I close my eyes and embrace the comfort I feel when he squeezes it.

"Well, ain't this lookin' cozy?" I jolt awake when I see Cole's wife standing in front of me with her hand on her hip and a judgmental look on her face. Then I realize what she's judging me for. I got my arm wrapped around Everleigh's shoulders, and she's tucked her body right into me. I have to close my eyes and reopen them to check I'm seeing things right.

"Savannah, what are you doin' here? I thought Garrett told you girls to—"

"I'm digging you out of a hole," she tells me, not even trying to hide the way her eyes flit over my bare torso. "I gotta hand it to ya, Mitch, you're packing for an old guy. Now, what you got to eat in this place?" She pats the neat bump that's sticking out over the top of her jeans and makes her way over to the kitchen. While I carefully stir Everleigh awake.

I don't know how we ended up like this, but the girl looks cute as hell when she's sleeping.

"Evy, darlin', you gotta wake up."

"Huh!" She gasps when she sees how close we are and I hold my hands up so she can see I'm respecting her boundaries. "We must've fallen asleep," I tell her, still wondering what the fuck Savannah's doing here.

"I'm sorry." Everleigh leaps up from the couch and when she sees the stranger routing through our kitchen cupboards, she looks even more daunted.

"Everleigh, this is Savannah," I explain quickly so she doesn't panic. "She's married to Cole, and she's here to..." I turn back to look at her. "What *are* ya here for?"

"I'm here because Josie's sick and Garrett needs you back at the ranch. Do you have any chocolate sauce I can put on these?" She tips some Cheerios into a bowl.

"I appreciate that, Sav, but—"

"Mitch, Garrett *really* needs to see you." The glare she gives me warns me that it's important. "I promise, me and Everleigh here will be just fine, now get yourself gone." She looks me up and down and when she winks at me, I quickly shove on my jeans and pull on a shirt.

"You okay with this?" I check, knowing how hard it is for Everleigh to be around people she doesn't know.

"Go, I'll be fine," she assures me, still looking unnerved by the fact we woke up together.

"Okay, I'll be back soon as I can." I move in to touch her the same as I did last night, but think better of it when I see how overwhelmed she's looking.

"Behave." I point at Savannah, before lifting up my hat and quickly heading out the door.

"What time ya call this?" Garrett smirks as I park my truck up beside his. He's already in his driver's seat looking ready to roll.

"I was... It was a long night, and what the *fuck* were you thinkin' sendin' Savannah up to the cabin?"

"Didn't she tell ya? Josie's sick."

"Yeah she told me, but, Savannah? *Really?* Don't ya think she's a little too much for Everleigh?"

"Well, we were all outta options. Maisie's still shaken up from the package she opened up yesterday and Leia had to take Dalton to get his shots."

"Hell, I think Finn or Tate would've been a better option than Savannah." I roll my eyes. I think highly of the girl, she's sure done a lotta good for Cole, but she's intrusive and has no filter. That's gonna be hard for Everleigh to handle.

"So where we goin' that's so urgent?" I ask, getting in beside him.

"We are goin' to pay a visit to Bianca Mason," he points out as he starts the engine.

"Are you mad?" I look across at him in shock.

"No, I'm attackin' this head-on." He stops himself when he realizes his choice of words is insensitive. "I mean, if she sent me Bucky Hall's head as a threat, I want her to know that she's gonna have to try harder."

He lifts a napkin-covered dish off the console and places it in my hand.

"What the hell's this?" I look down at it.

"That, Mitch, is a pie. I had Maisie make it so we can take it to Mrs. Mason and welcome her to *my* peaceful little town."

"You have got to be jokin'?" I shake my head, and the grin he directs back at me tells me he ain't. "And why do I have to come along to this doozy?" I question him.

"Because it was you who taught me, when I was five years old, that a man should never hurt a woman. I've got through my whole life never lettin' ya down but that bitch made my wife cry. You're comin' along to keep me in the good Lord's graces."

"Garrett, I think you got struck off His graces a long time ago." I shake my head, clutching hold of the fuckin' pie while he pulls out the drive.

"Mrs. Mason is very busy," the housekeeper who opens the door informs us.

"I'm sure she is, but you run along and you tell her that Mayor Carson's here to see her, anyway." Garrett doesn't wait for an invite as he steps over the threshold and I follow him, watching as he studies the foyer like he's never been here before.

"I see she wasted no time in redecoratin'," he says under his breath while we wait.

"Mayor Carson, what an honor." We both turn around when the clipped, female voice comes from behind us. Bianca Mason has pointy features much like her brother. She's dressed in a navy, pinstripe, pantsuit and heels that add a foot to her tiny frame. Her long, red hair is too vibrant to be natural and she has it pinned up tight on top of her head like it's the only thing holding up her fake-assed smile.

"I don't think there's any need for familiarities, we're practically neighbors." Garrett smiles as he holds out his hand for her to shake. She takes it and I see the tension in her knuckles as she squeezes.

"Here." He reaches over, takes the pie I'm holding out my hands, and offers it to her. "My wife insisted that I bring you somethin' to welcome you to town."

"How sweet." She smiles through her tight lips as she takes it. "I hear you keep your wife busy back at the homestead, three little ones must be a lot for her to handle." She twists her lips as if she's struggling to keep them elevated.

"And yet, she makes it look easy," Garrett smirks. "I hope you enjoy that pie," he gestures his eyes down at it. "Ain't nothin' better than locally sourced ingredients, we just so happened to have a delivery to the ranch yesterday," he informs her in a voice so full of charm that it covers up his rage.

"I'm sure it will be delicious." She passes it over to her housekeeper.

"Well, me and Mitch here just wanted to let you know that if ya need anythin', you can give us a call. Folk in this town look out for each other." He makes that last part sound like a threat as he heads for the door to see himself out.

"And did you extend that *kindness* to my brother and nephews?" Her question stops him in his tracks and when he turns back to face her, there's an arrogant snarl on his lips.

"I extend my kindness to anyone who wants to help my town flourish."

"*Your* town?" She lets out a tiny but very condescending laugh and I feel the tension building in Garrett.

"He's the mayor, ain't he?" I step in before he loses his shit. "And you're welcome here, ma'am." I look up at the wall where there's a huge portrait of her with her husband and two teenagers that I assume are her kids. "You all are." I make sure she sees the threat in my eyes before I lift my hat to her and then move past Garrett, opening the door for us to leave.

Garrett holds her stare for a good few seconds before he follows me out and I wait until we're inside the truck before I speak.

"You didn't really put any of Bucky Hall in that pie, did ya?" I check.

"What kinda sick fuck d'ya think I am?" Garrett starts the engine.

"Well, I could tell ya some stories." My answer seems to lighten his mood and we both laugh as we pull away. Seeing the smile back on his face calms my nerves, but it does nothing to help the problem that I got back home.

"So, what do you do around here all day?" The girl finishes her bowl and then moves into the living area, slumping herself onto the couch where I woke up beside Mitch this morning. I still can't believe that happened, but all I seem to be able to focus on is the fact I didn't have any nightmares. I slept without my memories haunting me.

"Ummm, well, I prepare dinner for when Mitch gets home, I watch some TV, and sometimes I read." I lift up the book I'm getting through for the third time since I've been here.

"You read this?" Savannah doesn't look impressed when she lifts up the worn copy of Moby Dick.

"Quite a few times, that and the Secret Garden are the only books here."

"You know, if you need anything, all you have to do is ask. Me and the girls have been looking forward to meeting you," she assures me.

"I appreciate that. And I don't want you to think I'm rude but—"

"You don't have to explain, we all understand," she cuts me off and I smile at her, despite not entirely believing what she says. I'm sure they would feel just as awkward around me as Josie does.

"So, you and Mitch?" I can tell she's trying far too hard to stop herself from grinning, and I don't know how to answer her. I don't know what to think of what happened just now myself. I can't remember the last time I slept without Solomon or Abraham creeping into my head and turning everything black again.

"Mitch is a very kind man." I shrug, not wanting to talk about something so private with a stranger.

"And he's hot as *fuck*," she points out.

"He's handsome, and he's patient. He's really good at playing the guitar too, you should hear him, sometimes he even sings an—"

"Oh, girl, you got it bad." Her head shakes and laughs.

"Got what bad?" I stare at her in confusion.

"The hots for Mitch, and I can't blame you, he's good for his age."

"He's not *that* old." I realize how defensive I'm sounding and decide I need to be much more guarded, this girl doesn't make it easy though.

Of course, I like Mitch, he's been so kind to me since I came here, and yes he's nice to look at, too. I've never really considered his age to be an issue. I actually like his gray hair and beard, I couldn't imagine it being any other color.

"I don't think age matters at all. If you like someone and they treat you right, no difference between you should matter." Savannah shrugs and I take in what she says. Just for a second, I imagine that our ages would be the only obstacle stopping us from going beyond what we are.

I know nothing about normal relationships, I barely know anything about the normal world. Up until a few days ago, I was content with that. Now, suddenly it seems like a curse that I want to break free from.

"I don't think it will ever be that simple with me," I tell her the sad but honest truth, which surprises me. Something about the way she is makes me feel like I can speak what's on my mind without it being judged or analyzed.

"Nothing around here is ever simple, and nothing great comes without taking a little risk. Don't rule anything out," she tells me.

"Mitch has a scar on his chest, where did it come from?" I blurt out curiously, remembering those bumpy letters I felt under my fingertips.

"You mean the brand?" Savannah bites her lip awkwardly. "I'm not really sure how much I'm supposed to tell you. I think it's best you ask Mitch yourself."

"Did someone hurt him, too?" I think about my own scars, the permanent reminder of the pain I suffered, and hate to think about him suffering too.

"Hurt him? Honey, he wasn't forced to have that done to him, he earned it. I know it's all kinds of strange but you gotta look at the brand as a lifestyle choice," she explains, and while I try my best to understand, none of it makes sense.

"So he wanted that?"

"Like I said, it's best you talk to him, and not just to ask about the brand. You should tell him how you feel... I'm sorry, I have to go pee." She rolls her eyes and quickly gets up to make her way to the bathroom. I sit in the silence and stare at the blanket that's on the couch beside me.

It may not seem like a big deal to most people that I let Mitch hold me last night while I slept a deep, wonderful sleep without fear and torment, but to me, it's huge progress. I don't know if Mitch shares the same kind of feelings that I do, but I like the idea of offering him more. I'd like him to hold me like that every night.

I get up and head into my room, picking up my journal and taking the pen that's on the nightstand, hoping I can speed this progress up a little bit more.

The thunder rumbles heavily and rain has been dripping through the gap in the door, trickling down the step for hours. I watch each of those drips form a puddle, until the light from outside fades and I get sent back into the blackness.

The hatch creaks open a few hours after sunset and as Abraham cautiously takes the stairs, holding the lantern in his hand, I will for him to slip and break his neck.

"Hello, Everleigh." His voice comes out powerful yet calm, just like it does when he gives his sermon on a Sunday. "I hope Solomon has been keeping you well."

I nod my head but keep my eyes on the floor. I can't tell him about the way Solomon touches me when he tends to me. I fear them both far too much.

"We have been unable to locate your sister. Do you know where she might be?" Abraham asks, moving closer to me and gripping my chin so I have no choice but to look at him.

"I swear that I don't know. Please let me go home," I beg, watching his old, wrinkled face turn blurry through my tears.

"My dear girl, you are home." He plants a kiss on my forehead. "The Lord needs Addison's repentance. Your sister was bound to me, she carries my seed in her womb and she has endangered herself and my child by leaving," he informs me, his tone is still calm, but I feel the force of his rage burning through his eyes.

"I had no idea she was going to run. I promise. You have to

believe me. Please let me speak to my parents." If this man hears the voice of God, surely He must be telling him to be merciful.

"Your father is ashamed. He knows that his daughter has failed him and he is prepared to offer you as the sacrifice."

"The sacrifice? To what?" My legs are shaking, struggling to hold me up.

"I lost a wife." His hand rests on my shoulder and he peers down at my dirty nightdress with a sick smile on his lips.

"You will serve me as she was expected to, and you will be punished for her sins every day until she returns to be punished for them herself." He spins my body so I'm facing away from him, slamming me front first into the cold, damp wall, and when his rough hands lift up my nightdress I start to cry.

"Please don't," I plead with him when his fingers start to knead at my flesh, groping and pinching at my skin.

"You are here to service me, Everleigh." He bears his weight against me, pressing me tighter against the brickwork. Something hard rests between my ass cheeks and I shudder at the thought of what it could be. I know what happens when a man lies with a woman. I know that him putting himself inside her is what causes her to get pregnant.

"Sir, I can't have a child. Not down here."

"A child?" He scoffs a cruel laugh at me. "A child?" His voice becomes louder and echoes from the walls. "My dear girl, you will not be getting a child." I feel my shoulders sag with relief. "You are not the chosen one, only those chosen by our almighty Lord receive such rewards. Like I said, you are here to service me." I try my best to think of how, and when I hear him spit and feel something heavy press against my back passage, I'm not prepared for what comes next...

. . .

I shut the journal and put it away when I feel that cold shiver start to creep over my skin. Pulling myself back together I head out the bedroom and find Savannah sitting in the living room stroking her hand over her stomach.

"There you are. I was wondering where you got to." She raises her smile up to me.

"Are you okay?" I check, noticing how she's cradling her tummy, it's obvious that she's expecting.

"Yeah, we're great, she's just having a little fidget in there." She looks down at her bump proudly. "Cole sits for hours at night with his hand over me trying to feel her, but she's most active when he's out working. I swear his voice just soothes her off to sleep."

"How do you know it's a girl?" I sit beside her and ask out of curiosity.

"Because I'm impatient and I had to know. The sonographer had written it down on a piece of paper so me and Cole could decide together when we found out, but I ripped open that envelope before we even got in the truck."

"Sonographer?" I try to keep up, there are so many terms I have to learn.

"Sorry, I forgot you lived on another planet." She laughs. "The doctors have a machine that allows them to look inside you and check that the baby is doing okay."

"That's amazing." I learn more every day about how incredible the world I've been sheltered from is.

"She's off again, do you wanna feel?" Savannah looks at me hopefully and I nod my head because I really do. I slowly stretch out my hand, placing it on her tummy, and when I feel a little wave move under my palm, I smile.

"Wow."

"She's strong, and she's gonna need to be. I'll bet her daddy will have her on a horse before she can walk."

"And your husband, he treats you right?" I check, suddenly feeling a sense of protection over this girl and the child that wriggles inside her.

"Everleigh, here, *all* the men treat their women right. They protect us, they love us and they would never hurt us." She places her hand over mine.

"Mitch is the same. He may come across as scary sometimes and he can be a miserable old coot, but he has a heart as big as his... you know." She winks at me and makes me blush.

We both turn our heads and look toward the door when we hear a truck pull up. "You should talk to him, tell him how you feel. I saw the look on his face this morning, and I heard the way he spoke to you. I've never heard that man speak so softly in all the time I've been here." She stands up and makes her way to the door. "Don't waste all this wonderful time you have now you're free, looking back. If you do, you might as well be back wherever you came from." I freeze when she unexpectedly kisses me on the cheek. I'm not used to human affection, but instead of panicking I smile.

"Thank you," I call after her before she sees herself out.

"Hey, darlin." Mitch strolls in as she leaves, and when I see him I get this overpowering urge to run at him and throw my arms around his neck. Though I refrain, staying rooted to the spot and suddenly realizing that I've spent the whole time he's been gone distracted by Savannah.

"Oh, no. It must be lunchtime, I haven't prepared anything." I rush to the kitchen to see what I can put together. Mitch left here without having any breakfast, he must be starving.

"Whoa, steady up. It's fine, I can make myself a sandwich." He frowns at me.

"No, I'll make something better, you didn't eat breakfast.

We have some leftover beef, I can make some pastry for a pie. It won't take—"

"NO!" He raises his voice to interrupt me, and his skin looks a little paler than usual. "No pie." He lowers his tone again, looking repulsed by the idea.

"I'll just make us a sandwich." He smiles to assure me that everything's okay, but the way my heart flutters in response to it makes me certain that things are going to get complicated.

It's way past the time that she usually goes to bed, and I notice the way her eyes keep flicking away from the TV screen over to me like she has something on her mind.

"Ya have fun with Savannah today?" I ask, knowing how spirited Cole's woman can be.

"We had a great time. I felt her baby move." She smiles excitedly.

"I'm glad to hear that. She can be loud and outspoken, but she's got her heart in the right place," I tell her, hoping that maybe this could be the start of her letting the girls get closer.

"She was kind to me." Everleigh nods her head, looking deep in thought.

"Well, that's all that matters." I settle back into my chair and drink my beer.

"Mitch..." She sits up a little straighter, suddenly seeming nervous.

"I want to speak about what happened last night, and this morning." She clears her throat, and as I watch the heat creep up her neck I feel bad for the fact it's getting my dick hard.

"Look, darlin', I never meant to cross any bound—"

"I liked it." She shocks the hell outta me when her voice blurts over the top of mine.

Her eyes shut tight as if she's just confessed some kinda sin, and I know there's an inappropriate grin picking up on my face because I'm really struggling to keep it down.

"I felt safe like they couldn't get me, and I..."

"You didn't have any bad dreams," I finish her sentence for her when I think back to how peaceful she looked in my arms.

"I hate going back there." A tear slips over her cheek, and I feel that knot of anger in my stomach ball up tighter when I think about the asshole that did this to her.

"They can't get ya here, *they* don't even exist anymore. Listen..." I move across and sit on the couch beside her. "You need to leave everything that happened at that place back there with it. You have a chance of a new life."

"Here, with you?" She looks up at me with those big, blue eyes and I swear they wrap a chain around my heart.

"Wherever you want it." I've got used to coming home to her and having her around. I've even got used to the screaming she does while she sleeps. It feels good to be her protector, to be the voice that calls her back from the dark. Up until now, the girl's been so closed off I never even thought about how it might feel to lose her.

"I like it here, and I like you." She lays her hand over mine, and suddenly I'm the one who's nervous. I don't know what this is, or if she's thinking the same way as me. I'm old enough to be the girl's father. Maybe she sees me like one, and I don't wanna be her fuckin' daddy.

"This place is gonna be your home for as long as you need it," I assure her of the one thing I can guarantee.

"And you, will you always be here?" she asks.

I look down to where our hands touch, and having her trust

feels like the most precious gift in the world. I wanna protect that too.

"Until the day you tell me not to be." I smile at her, stroking over her skin with my thumb and praying to God that day never comes, because whatever brought this pretty, vulnerable girl into my life, seems to have suddenly given me my purpose.

"If I asked you to lay beside me again tonight, would you?" she asks, her eyelashes fluttering and her skin turning pink.

"Sweetheart, I wouldn't deny you a damn thing." I smile.

She grips hold of my hand as she stands up, and I look up at her, wondering how the fuck something so beautiful and innocent could seek her comfort from a man like me.

"I'm going to change into my nightdress, I'll call you in when I'm ready." She blushes before she releases me and moves toward her room.

I wait until she closes the door before I let go of my fuckin' breath.

I don't know what's happening here, but it feels intense, and dare I say it, *scary*. I'd forgotten what fear felt like until I met her.

I should tell her that me lying beside her is a bad idea, that the thoughts that go through my mind can sometimes get real unholy, but the idea of me being the person who makes her feel safe has me getting on my feet when she opens the door and smiles at me again.

Stepping toward her, she follows me with her eyes when I pass her at the door.

"You got a side you prefer?" I ask as I take off my jeans. This girl's seen me in my boxers before so I figure she won't mind.

"No." She shakes her head as she takes her hair out of its braid and timidly watches me strip outta the shirt I'm wearing. I keep on the white tee that I've got on underneath, and after I move around the bed, so I'm lying closest to the door, I pull back the covers and get in.

I try not to stare at her in the long, cotton gown that falls all the way to her ankles, and when she sinks to her knees beside the bed and presses her palms together I watch in fascination as she says her prayers.

"God bless Mitch for being my protection. God bless the Carson family for allowing me to be here. God bless the Dirty Souls for saving me, and God bless my sister." Her voice weakens and I see another tear streak down her face before she opens her eyes and stands back on her feet.

"You say your prayers every night, darlin'?" I ask, wonderin' how the hell she just made talkin' to God look so damn hot.

"Every night," she assures me as she joins me under the covers, leaving a very respectable gap between us.

"And do you always—"

"You're always in them," she answers the question before I can finish it.

"That's kind of ya, but I think I'm long past savin'." I chuckle to myself but hold on to the warm, comforting feeling of knowing I'm in her prayers.

"No one's past saving, I'm proof of that." There's hope in the smile she makes for me. "Do you want to know a secret?" She angles her body so it's facing me.

"Of course." I frown suspiciously. I wanna know everything about her, even all the parts that made her broken. Maybe then I could fix her.

"I used to hate God. I used to wonder why He demanded such cruel things. I didn't praise Him, I feared Him," she admits.

"And now?" I study her.

"Now I realize you were right. God wasn't speaking

through those men. They used His name, and our faith in it, to fulfill their own desires."

"And your sister? You mentioned her in your prayers there. Have you stopped hating her too?" Maybe if she has, she'll wanna be reunited with her, and it proves how selfish I've become that I don't want that to happen.

"I don't hate Addison, at least I don't think I do. To hate her would be selfish. I just..." She closes her eyes and shakes her head. "I can't explain it." I realize that she's pushing herself too hard.

"Hey, you don't have to explain anythin' to me, I was just being curious," I assure her. "Just get yourself some sleep."

To lean in and kiss those pretty, rose-colored lips would be the most natural thing in the world right now, but I ignore all my urges and twist my body to turn off the lamp.

"Wait... I need that to stay on. I don't like the dark." She stops me.

"Sure." I look back over my shoulder at her before resting back on my pillow and staring up at the ceiling. Everleigh rolls onto her side, facing away from me and I already know that lying this close to her is gonna make for a long night.

"Mitch," she whispers my name after a few minutes of silence.

"Yeah, darlin'?"

"Tell me one of your memories, a happy one." She speaks softly, and staring at the back of her head makes me wanna stroke my fingers through her hair. It's grown so long since she's been here and it looks real soft.

"Okay." I search around in my head and try to come up with something that will make her laugh. I don't think I've ever heard her laugh before.

"There was this one time when Dalton was younger. I'd taken him to the rodeo, and he came home sure that he was gonna be a bull rider. The next morning, he got up early and decided to get himself practicin', put himself in the pen with a bull we were waiting to put out to pasture. We called him Old Ronnie because he was a grumpy, old fucker like Old Man Mason." I smile to myself when I remember the kid's enthusiasm.

"And how did he do?" she asks, sounding intrigued.

"He didn't. Old Ronnie just kept charging him around the pen, eventually the grumpy, old bastard pinned him into a corner and tossed him out. Dalton took a horn to the ass cheek as a hard lesson, and never tried to be a bull rider again."

Her shoulders start to shake and the sound that comes outta her mouth is addictive.

"Poor kid could barely sit down for a month." I laugh a little too, until that sting that reminds me I'll never see him again hits.

"Thank you." She closes her eyes and pulls the covers up to her chin, and as I lay here looking at her, thinking about how perfect she is, I wonder if maybe she could be the person who takes that sting away.

CHAPTER 10

EVERLEIGH

The sun peeking through the gap in the curtains warms my face and wakes me up. Warm breath and something bristly tickles my neck, and when I look down and see the forearm wrapped around my middle, I smile. Taking a look over my shoulder I realize Mitch is still sleeping, and although his hold on me is tight and constricting, I don't mind it at all.

I lie with my eyes open, with his chest rising and falling against my back, and take comfort in how it feels. Being close to Mitch is something I'm rapidly getting attached to, and I don't know if it's a good thing.

The world beyond these walls is vast and scary. I'm detached from it but he's not. I don't want to be the reason he misses out on doing all the normal things his friends do.

"Mornin'." His low, raspy voice whispers into my ear and I breathe it in like it's fresh air.

"I didn't mean to—" He goes to move his arm away.

"It's fine." I rest my hand over it to keep it where it is, and when I feel him tense I wonder if it's out of frustration or fear.

"It's Sunday. You don't have to rush off, do you?"

"No, I don't." I don't turn around, but I can imagine the

smile on his face. The half amused, half trying not to be, smile that always warms the pit of my stomach.

"I slept again last night, no nightmares." I spin around so I can see what his reaction to that is.

"That's good to hear." His Adam's apple sticks out as he swallows heavily, and I can't help noticing how his eyes are fixed on my lips.

"Look, Mitch, I know this arrangement is odd. All of it is, but—"

"If it's what ya need, I'm here for it," he interrupts me.

"I'd just hate to think that there was a person out there that I was taking you away from." I don't even want to imagine that could be the case but I have to be sure.

"There ain't no person." His jaw tenses.

"But there could be." I turn my body to face him properly. "Mitch, you're a good man. Every night, you come to me when you could be out—"

"I've had my days of bein' out. I can promise ya that comin' home to you is exactly where I wanna be. One day, who knows, we might go out together." I see a little sparkle of hope in his eyes, and even though the thought of it terrifies me I like the idea of making him happy.

"Maybe." I shrug, knowing that day is a long way off. I don't feel comfortable stepping out into the yard to hang out washing, let alone face up to civilization.

"Everythin' at your pace, you know that," he assures me.

"What is this?" I shake my head and laugh nervously. "We lie together like a master and his wife, but we're not..." I trail off, not knowing what I'm trying to get at.

"What we have here, Everleigh, is a man who cares greatly for a woman and wants to save her from her past. You had no choices where ya came from, here you have nothin' *but* choices.

I'll lie like this with ya every night for as long as you need me to, and I expect nothin' for it."

"You're a good man," I tell him, wondering if the butterflies I get in my stomach every time I hear his deep, gravelly voice will ever fade away. "I want to give you more."

Suddenly he looks panicked and he quickly slides away from me to climb out of bed.

"Where are you going?" I sit up.

"I just remembered Wade wants me to take the horse he's trainin' out for a stretch alongside JD. I won't be gone long, but I could call Josie. I'm sure she's better."

"It's fine, I don't need her, not if you won't be long." I feel a little disappointed that he has to leave, and I can't help wondering if it's because of what I said. Lying beside him felt nice, and not at all awkward like it should have. I wanted to give him some indication of my feelings so maybe I could get a clue about what he's thinking.

"You want me to make us some breakfast?" I climb out of bed myself, suddenly desperate for him to stay a little longer.

"No, sooner I can get gone, the sooner I can get back. I just... I should get goin'." He picks up his jeans from the floor and rushes out the room. Seeing him so eager to get away from me puts a sick feeling in my stomach and makes me want to chase after him.

I hear the front door click five minutes later and when I step out into the kitchen and see my journal resting on the table, I open it and see my handwriting staring back up at me. I don't want to read the words that I wrote yesterday, it would be a step backward. I have to focus on moving forward. My therapist was right, writing them down is clearing my head and allowing some space. Space that is currently being occupied by a certain cowboy who I want so badly to be normal for.

I sit at the table and pick up the pen, deciding to free up a little more space for him.

The door opens and when Solomon treads carefully down the stairs, I see the tray balanced on his hand and my stomach instantly grumbles. Abraham feeds me twice a day, and it's always stale bread or tasteless gruel. I see fresh fruit on a plate that's on the tray and what looks a lot like a slice of cake.

"Morning, little dove." He smiles as he places it on the floor, just out of the bounds that my shackles allow me to stretch to.

"Please, can you empty my bucket?" I refuse to look at the food he's brought down here to tease me with. I'd much rather focus on the bucket that's overflowing with my body waste.

"All in good time." He steps up in front of me.

"My father and a few of the elders have gone teaching, he's left me in charge of the home," he explains, sounding mighty proud of himself.

"This was left over from supper." He steps aside so he isn't blocking the tray. "I was thinking you might like it." I resist the urge to charge at it like a rabid dog and remain still.

"Would you like the food, little dove?" he asks me softly, and I nod my head as my mouth becomes dry and desperate.

"Of course, you do. My father treats you so poorly, you've lost all the color from your cheeks." His thumb slides over my face and makes me hold my breath.

"You've lost all those pretty curves you had." He uses my hair to drag me up onto my feet. "I used to imagine squeezing those juicy, round tits you had in my palm, but now..." He looks down at my chest and sniggers to himself.

"I want to give you the food, Everleigh, I want to give it to you so badly." He forces me back against the wall and lets me

feel the weight of his body against me. "But you have to give me a little something first."

"Please, don't." *I shake my head because I'm exhausted. Abraham comes down here at least every other day and he ruts into me from behind like an animal. My back hole constantly throbs from his assault, and no time seems to have passed at all since he last took me.*

"My father tells me how you hate it. He says he has to gag you because your screams are so deafening." *He laughs as if my misery is a joke between him and his father.*

"I don't want you to hate the things I do to you. I want you to take pleasure in them." *He slowly starts to raise my nightdress.*

"No, please." *I shake my head.*

"He tells me you're still unbroken. It can be both of our first times, just like it was supposed to be." *He reaches into the front of his pants and takes out his manhood, pulling it through his fist and ensuring the tip of it touches against me.*

"You feel that, little dove? It's all for you." *He rubs it against me as his tongue slides over my cheek.*

"Please, don't."

"I'll make it nice for you, you can take pleasure from it. The screams Nancy makes for Dad, sometimes, don't sound painful. The other wives whisper about her behind her back, they say she enjoys him, and you will enjoy me." *He shoves his free hand between my legs to force them apart.*

"We can't, your father said I wasn't chosen. I'm not to bear a child."

He ignores me as he gets himself in line with my entrance, and with one hand gripped under my jaw, he uses the other to steer himself inside me.

I scream when he uses all his force to penetrate me, his face distorted and frustrated as he struggles to get past my barrier.

"Loosen up, you're too tense," he growls in frustration.

"I can't." I shake my head as he lifts my feet off the ground and anchors them around his thick-set hips. He spits onto his hand and uses his saliva to coat his cock before he forces it inside me again, and I scream as he prods into me, over and over until I feel a sharp pain rip through my stomach.

"That's a girl," he grunts as he continues pumping himself inside me.

The pain is just as excruciating as when his father takes me, and all I can do is look over his shoulder at the plate of food and watch the flies settle on the juicy fruit.

"You're mine, Everleigh. He may come and take you, but this part of you belongs to me." Solomon moans and I'm grateful that he doesn't last anywhere near as long as his father does.

His soft cock eventually slips out of me and after he wipes my blood off it, he examines his hand proudly.

"We must keep this our secret. I'd hate to think how father would punish you if he found out." He smiles as he wipes his hand clean on my dirty nightgown.

"You enjoyed that, didn't you?" He backs away, tucking himself inside his pants. "I hear it only hurts the first time. Next time, you'll feel nothing but pleasure." He kicks the plate forward to me so it's within my reach and I'm too hungry to be stubborn. I dive for it, lifting a slice of apple to my lips, but he stops me with a shake of his head.

"No hands. I want to see you eat like a dog, while my cum drips out of you." He walks around me and lifts my hips so I'm on all fours. And I close my eyes in shame.

I want to cry. I want to scream. I want to hurt the ugly bastard who feeds on my humiliation. But I'm hungry and so I do as he says. Lowering my head and eating his offerings like an animal.

"You look so pretty," he tells me, crouching down beside me

and tilting his head back to look between my legs. Just like he said, I feel his seed running out of me, and it takes the sweetness out of the strawberry I'm eating

"We're going to have many secrets together, little dove," he tells me, stroking my hair as I continue to force down the food in front of me.

"Hope I'm not interrupting anything?" The door barges open and Savannah strolls in, carrying with her a stack of books.

"Not at all." I slam the journal closed.

"I've been thinking about those awful books you've been stuck reading, and I hooked you up." She places her pile on the table in front of me.

"What are they?" I lift up the top one and blush when I see that the guy on the cover has his shirt open. He's got strong chest muscles like Mitch, but he's missing the hair that covers them that I like.

"Maisie calls it romance, I call it smut. But the stories are good. These men know how to treat their women, and there's nothing like a good, old love story to restore your faith in humanity," she points out.

"Well, I appreciate it." I smile up at her, realizing that I'm genuinely happy to see her. It feels like another step forward.

"You're welcome. Once a month, me, Leia, and Maisie get together and talk about a book we read together. We started off with Little Women but after I had my turn to make the selection, we never went back." She winks as she heads over to the stove and picks up the kettle.

"Are you staying?" I ask, hoping that she is. Savannah's company makes the time pass much faster.

"I only got half an hour, I promised Leia I'd look after Dalton while she goes out to lunch with her mom and sister.

Her and her mother don't really get on. If I was her I wouldn't go at all, but she does it for Karina." Savannah bustles around the kitchen and makes me a coffee while I sit and listen to her ranting.

I wonder if this is what normal is like. It doesn't feel as if Savannah is here because she has to look after me, or because she's been told to. I really think she chose to come out here and spend time with me. I can't help feeling disappointed when she realizes that she's lost track of time and has to go.

I see her to the door, then notice what a beautiful day we're having and I decide to push another one of my boundaries. Picking up one of the books she brought me, I take a deep breath and head on out to the porch so I can read it.

I never venture out here unless I have to put out laundry or hang the lantern for Mitch when he's home late. It sounds stupid considering the man has spent his whole life living on this ranch, but there is nothing but hills and fields surrounding this cabin. I worry every time he leaves that he won't find his way home to me, and that fear has me stepping out the door and lighting the lantern, even if it's dark.

I take the bench seat that's under the kitchen window and get started on the book, feeling proud of what I'm achieving, even if my steps are small.

CHAPTER 11

MITCH

I feel bad for leaving the way I did, but seeing the way she looked at me and hearing her say she wanted to give me more, suddenly made me feel like a fraud. Sleeping beside her last night felt like torture, all I wanted to do was touch her again. To wrap her up in my arms and be that comfort she needs. I was just scared of pushing her too far.

Turns out, the second I switched off my body it let me down and did it anyway.

Waking up beside her this morning felt like the kinda thing I wanna do for the rest of my life. But I have to remember that this girl only sees the man who steps through the door at night. She doesn't know about the souls I got on my conscience or the secrets I keep that could set Hell ablaze.

I've seen some of the shit the Carson women have been through because of who they are and what their men do. The cost of loving a branded man is a tough one to pay, and Everleigh has been through far too much to survive that.

I should be helping her heal so she can move on and find herself some happiness outta this life, instead, I find myself fantasizing about *being* that happiness. I want to be the dream inside her nightmare and the hope for her future, and that's real selfish of me.

I saddle up JD and tether up the horse, Wade's been training, beside us before I head out the gate. She seems a lot better than the last time I took her out, and JD is a great horse to learn from. Though I'm sure I don't need to tell Wade that she's gonna be a lost cause when it comes to driving cattle. She's far too skittish.

I ride a few miles, trying to get Everleigh outta my head, and all I feel is guilt for the way I left this morning. She looked so happy when I woke up, she wasn't scared by the fact I was holding her. In fact, she made sure I didn't pull away. I ruined it all by getting weird on her.

Everleigh doesn't need me acting like a love-sick teenager around her. She needs a man. One who ain't scared to feel, and ain't scared to show her those feelings. It's gonna take time for her to adjust to this life, and she's got a long way to go before she heals. I wanna be there for her every step of it. I've never felt about a female this strongly and I'm stuck between a rock and a hard place and right and wrong. My conscience tells me that letting her go would be the kind and decent thing to do, but I've never been good at listening to that.

I change my direction and head toward the cabin, knowing I need to apologize to her. She's gonna be alone and overthinking. I hate the idea of her thinking she did something wrong. I've spent the past few years dishing out advice to the boys, tellin' 'em they gotta tell their girls how they feel, and I think it's high time I take my own advice. I should let her know I'm scared, let her know that I want the more that she's offering but I'm too damn afraid to take it.

I have to check twice when the cabin comes into view and I see Everleigh sitting out on the porch. She hardly ever leaves the cabin, which concerns me, so to see her out in the fresh air comes as a welcomed surprise.

She's reading a book and quickly places it down when she notices me riding toward her.

"Hey." She stands up looking a little flustered, and I wonder if it's because of how I left her earlier. I don't want her to start feeling uncomfortable around me like she did when she first got here.

"I need to talk to you." I tether the horses to the porch rail and step in front of her.

"She's beautiful." Everleigh's attention moves past me and to the horse. She reaches out her hand to touch her and I'm about to warn that she gets freaked out easily, but I stop when I notice how the horse bows her head to invite Everleigh's touch.

"I've never seen one in real life." She makes the most beautiful giggle as the mare lifts her head and demands more of her attention.

"She's beautiful, alright." I stare at the girl and realize that everything I've just convinced myself of is wrong. I can't keep this girl here, trapped with an old man like me. Not when there's a whole world of beautiful out there for her to see.

"What did you want to talk about?" Everleigh turns to look at me with that pretty smile still on her face.

"I... I can't remember." I smile back sadly as I watch her focus back on the horse, stroking her nose over the railings and looking so perfect that my heart feels as if it's bleeding.

"How much d'ya want for the horse?" I ask Wade when I get back to the yard.

"What? That useless thing?" He stares back at me as if I've gone crazy.

"Yeah, ya heard right. How much?" I ask again.

"Mitch, she ain't good for nothin'. Unless you've worked some of that old cowboy magic with her."

"No, she's still scared of her own shadow, but I want her."

"Have you been day drinkin'?" He laughs at me.

"No, I just want the damn horse. Now, are ya givin' me an interview or making a deal?"

"You really want that fuckin' horse, don't ya?" He shakes his head and laughs.

"Yeah, I want it. Now, what's your price?"

"You can have her for what Cole paid." He still looks confused.

"Done." I take both horses into the stable and make sure they have water, then call over Hunter when I notice him mucking out the stable where Garrett keeps Thunder.

"How ya likin' it here?" I ask, watching him take the initiative and loosen my saddle so he can hang it on the wall.

"Well, aside from the flying heads, I'm likin' it. Tate taught me how to rope a calf, he said I've got natural talent. Just need practice. Hell, I'm even thinking about gettin' one of these bad boys for myself." He smacks the mare on her ass and almost jumps out his skin when she neighs back at him. "Just got to work on some funds." He looks a little spooked as he strokes her back to calm down, but he smiles at me all the same.

"No, ya don't. That horse ya rode out the other day? He's yours." I look over to Blaze who's over in the stall in the far corner.

"What? I can't accept that. It's a horse..." Hunter looks at me like I'm crazy.

"You can, and you will. I don't know if ya figured it yet, but ya can't be a cowboy without a ride."

"Is he yours too?" he asks.

"He belonged to my nephew." I swallow the lump in my

throat and it tastes fuckin' rotten. "He's a good horse, too good to be used as a spare." I fight back the tears that are threatening to come.

"I've heard about Dalton, I'm sorry." Hunter hangs his head outta respect.

"Don't be sorry, just accept the horse and take good care of him." I don't wanna be making no song and dance about it. I can tell Hunter's a good kid, he reminds me a little of Dalton, and having him around is proving to be handy.

"While you're at it, I need ya to take care of her too. Between us I want her ridden every day. She'll be a challenge, but you persevere with her." I go to stroke her nose like Everleigh did but she pulls away from me.

"Wade sell her?" Hunter looks surprised again.

"Yeah, he sold her. To me, and I need her to be reliable. I want her saddled up and ready by 5:30 every mornin' and if I ain't here, you jump on her and do the best ya can."

"I didn't know you trained horses." Hunter folds his arms over his chest.

"It's been a while, but you never lose your touch. Remember what I said. 5:30." I point at him before I leave.

When I get back to the cabin, Everleigh is sitting in my chair reading again and she greets me with that smile that I'm trying to convince myself doesn't belong to me. The last few days she's let her guard slip right down and I can't allow that to make me lose focus.

"I spoke to Skid earlier, he's gonna up your therapy sessions," I tell her, trying not to look at her. I need us to go back to having boundaries or letting her go will be too hard.

"What? That's crazy. I don't need more sessions. I'm getting better. I can feel it. I've even been writing in my journal. Don't you think what's happened between us is progre—"

"It's progress that's leadin' in the wrong direction," I snap at her, hearing the spite in my voice and hating how it sounds.

"I said I'd be here for you and I will be, but wakin' up the way we did this mornin'..." The volume in my voice tapers to a weak whisper. "It ain't right."

"It felt right," she hits back, and when I raise my eyes to take a glance at her, seeing how hurt she looks makes me wanna throw my fist at the wall.

"Yeah, well, just because somethin' feels right at the time, doesn't make it okay. It ain't proper for a man of my age to be lyin' in a bed with a girl of yours."

"Mitch, I'm..." She has to do some thinking on it. "I'm twenty-two years old. I'm not a child."

"I never said you were, but if people knew we were sharin' a bed, there would be talk of us—"

"Liking each other." She shocks me with how brash she's being. There's sarcasm in the smile that seems to have overridden her panic. "I *do* like you, Mitch. I like the way I feel when I'm around you and I like the way it felt when I woke up this morning," she admits, pulling back her shoulders and standing strong.

"This isn't up for negotiation, Everleigh. The sleepin' in the same bed thing has to stop." I put my foot down and storm out the door when I see her confidence shrink and her bottom lip start to wobble.

I have an outhouse to fix up into a stable.

I burst into tears as I watch him storm across the yard toward the shack on the other side of it. He must be angry because he kicks one of the rafters that's holding up the roof and makes the whole thing collapse.

I've been going over and over this morning in my head, trying to think of what I did wrong, and now seeing him so angry because of me, makes me want to cry.

Fear creeps its way into my chest and grips its hold. I don't know where we go from here because it doesn't feel as if we can go back. Living in the bunker was hell, but at least there I knew who I belonged to.

Since I was rescued I've been nothing but a burden, first to the Souls and now to Mitch too.

I wipe away my tears as I stand and watch the man compose himself. Then I laugh a sad, bitter laugh that only a person who's made a fool of themselves would know how to make.

I knew coming into this world that I'd be naïve to it, but how could I have thought that it was possible to have a future after what I endured? How did I picture a man wanting me after the damage that's been done, not just to my body, but inside my head?

I'm not pure of sin like Mitch thinks I am, my bones are riddled with it. My skin starts to itch when I think about the way Solomon used to touch me. I got through those times by telling myself that what he did to me was his way of sharing his love. He'd wanted me to be his, and what Addison did ruined that for him.

I knew I could never have loved Solomon, even if I was his wife. But I still took pity on him and what he lost.

Which is more than he ever did for me.

"You haven't bled in weeks?" Solomon's cock flops out of me and he stares at me with concern etched all over his face. I say nothing, just keep my eyes focused on the floor. He's right, I haven't bled for weeks and I know just as well as he does what that means.

"Everleigh, are you..."

"I think so," I answer, holding back my tears and admitting what I haven't allowed my head to contemplate.

"That's great news." He scrambles toward me, placing his hands over my filthy nightdress so his palm can cradle my concave stomach. His reaction may be unwelcome, but it also gives me hope. Knowing that I carry his child now might make me valuable enough for him to consider talking to his father. This baby could be my salvation.

"A blessing." I place my hand over his and forge a smile for him.

"A blessing, indeed." His dreamy smile remains in place while my body turns cold.

. . .

Mitch says nothing when he steps back inside the cabin a few hours later, and I take my journal and slide it under the cushion beside me. There's tension between us now and I hate it. More than anything, I hate the uncertainty of everything.

"What did I do wrong? At least tell me that." My voice comes out desperate and weak but I don't care. I need answers.

Mitch turns his head to look at me and all the harshness on his face fades when he sighs a long, heavy breath.

"You did nothin' wrong, nothin' at all. It was me who fucked up."

"How?" I shake my head, hoping he'll help me understand.

"By lettin' myself get carried away and wantin' somethin' I can't have." He comes toward me and crouches in front of me. "Everleigh, you're beautiful, and you're sweet, and despite everythin' you've been through there ain't nothin' but good in you."

"I know what you're gonna say but—"

"No, ya don't." He shakes his head and takes my hand in his. "I'm old, I'm stuck in my ways and I've found my place on this Earth to call home. You're young, you got a whole world out there to explore. You need to find your home, and I wanna make you better so you can do that—"

"So lie with me, hold me the way you did, because that's what makes me feel better." I stare deep into his eyes, willing for him to understand.

"I'm sorry, darlin' but ya have to understand. You can be the best man in the world, with all the right intentions; but when ya get that little piece of perfect that completes the puzzle, it can be very hard to let go of." He looks sad as his thumb brushes over my skin.

"This trust..." He looks down at where we touch. "Is the greatest, most precious gift anyone ever gave me. But I can't accept anythin' more than that." One of my tears drips onto his hand and we both watch it roll off. "There's a strong woman insida you, she's the only one who can free herself, and when that happens there's no way I'm gonna let her settle for this grumpy, old man who's had his day. The world's waitin' for ya, Everleigh." He raises my hand up to his mouth and kisses it before standing back up and heading toward the bathroom.

I pat my cheeks to dry them before I pull my journal back out from behind the cushion and this time what I write isn't a bad memory, it's an all-consuming emotion that I have to get out of my head and hope I can move on from.

I love him.

If I thought hearing her nightmares was torture before, I was wrong. Sitting on the other side of the door when I know how it feels to have her in my arms and make her better, feels like having your heart scooped outta your chest. I have to be cruel to be kind. I've let myself get carried away and forgot that my job was to look out for her through her journey, not become part of it. I grip my fists together when I hear more of her screams and bite down on my knuckles.

Knowing that I could be the one to take her pain away suddenly feels like a curse. If I go back into that room and give her what she needs it'll give her false hope. I can already feel that she's attached, she doesn't see a life beyond this cabin, and for an old guy like me, that would be easy to take advantage of. So I sit and I listen. I let her pain ring through my ears and wish there was another option to take it away.

The thought of another man comforting her almost makes me as sick to my stomach as the thoughts of the bastard who did this to her. And those are the kinda thoughts that I can't linger on.

Everleigh was not put on this earth to be mine, and it's sad and cruel that our paths crossed this way, because if they hadn't I'd never have had to learn the pain of letting her go.

"Come on, darlin', fight past it." I look up at the ceiling and whisper to myself. Willing it to be over for her. She can't rely on me, she needs to be able to leap back into the light all by herself, there's no other way for her to get strong.

"DON'T!" she screams. "DON'T DO THAT. PLEEASE!." She breaks into sobs that crack my heart right down the middle.

"No... No." The sound that comes next is too much to take. It's high-pitched and so full of terror that I'm done listening to the poor girl suffer.

I leap onto my feet and barge through the door to get to her. She's still got her eyes squeezed shut, her nightdress is clinging to her body from sweat, and I don't waste another second standing still

"Everleigh. Everleigh, it's me." I climb onto the bed beside her and wrap my arms around her body to stop her from shaking.

"Everleigh!" I call her name louder, and when she opens her eyes and sees me, she looks stunned as her panicked, little breaths get shorter.

"I'm here, you're with me. Ya ain't there, anymore," I whisper, pulling her onto my chest and pressing my lips into the top of her head. She was right about what she said earlier, nothing about this feels wrong, and as her hands cling to my arms like I'm all she has in this wretched world, I push any doubt in what I'm doing to the back of my mind so I can give her what she needs.

I wake up long before she does, and it gives me the opportunity to appreciate how beautiful she is. Now that her nightmares are over she looks peaceful, and it takes all my willpower not to lean over and let my mouth touch over hers. It's an intrusive thought that I shouldn't let in, and one that now it's there, I can't push away. My hand reaches over her and I carefully trace her lips with my finger, allowing myself to imagine how they'd feel against mine. Her eyes flicker open and catch me in the act, but I don't move, I stare right back at her, and when she softly kisses my fingertips it suddenly feels hard to breathe.

"You came to me?" She smiles.

"Of course, I did." I move my hand away and prop my head up on it. "It was a bad one, the worst I ever heard," I admit, feeling that gut-wrenching pain in my stomach when I recall listening to it.

"I'm sor—"

"No, no more apologies." I shake my head. "Darlin', this is a bad idea."

"Please don't send me away. I thought about what you said last night, about finding my home and, Mitch... What if my home is here with you? What if God intended us to find each other all along?"

"God wouldn't be so cruel." I laugh to myself, but she doesn't seem to find any humor in my words.

"All I know is that the thought of not being with you puts pain inside me." She holds her hand to her chest. "I want to prove to you that I'm not just here because I'm scared of what's out there. I want to find my limits and the only way I can do that is to push them." She looks so brave as she smiles up at me. "I need you to help me do that, Mitch."

"I'll help you in any way I can," I promise her. I've just decided that the risk of breaking my heart is worth the reward of fixing hers.

"And if I prove to you that I'm not here out of fear, will you accept that what we have between us can't be denied because of a silly thing like age?" she asks.

"I never denied that there was somethin' between us," I point out, taking a strand of her blonde hair in my finger and sliding it back behind her ear. "I just want you to have the best of what this life has to offer, and that ain't me, sweetheart."

She surprises me when her hand lifts up and slides it across my bristly jaw.

"I've had choices taken away from me my whole life. Let this one be mine." She smiles before snuggling her body back into mine.

"**H**as Solomon been feeding you extras?" Abraham prods his bony finger hard at my stomach, and I crouch over to protect the child that grows inside it. The ridge of my stomach is only tiny and would hardly be noticeable if the rest of me hadn't become skin and bone.

It's a miracle that something could survive within me. I never get fed properly. I'm beaten almost daily and I'm constantly forced to take Abraham's cock either in my ass or mouth. Just two days ago, Abraham smashed me against the wall so hard that I actually blacked out.

"Say the words." Abraham removes his belt like he always does and when I feel its cold buckle press against my backside, I prepare myself for what comes next.

"He will be gracious and forgive us our sins," I say the words he demands I speak.

"And..." he encourages me.

"Her sins will be punished, through Him, unto me." I flinch when the metal hits my skin, trying to hold back my cries. He drives his cock into my mouth as he leans over my back and continues to strike me, somehow hitting the same spot every time with the buckle and making the pain excruciating. He holds my head tight against him so I choke and splutter on him and when he fills my mouth with his seed, my stomach retches like I'm going to throw up.

"And you take her punishments so well." He pulls away from me and laughs as he slaps my cheek.

I want to scream at him, tell him that he repulses me and that I'm glad my sister got away from him. I can't imagine how she must have felt about carrying his child. I might not like Solomon all that much, but at least he can be kind. Abraham and his terrible breath and rotten teeth are far worse than any monster I've ever been told of.

He leaves me in the darkness and I lie on my side, stroking my hand over the tiny bump I've got. I know he or she won't stay a secret forever, and Solomon is going to have to do something to get us out of here soon, for his own sake, not just mine. He may not admit it, but he fears his father and he knows Abraham would be furious if he knew what he's been doing to me.

I've just finished being sick in the bucket when the hatch pulls open and I can't believe what I'm seeing when Magna follows in after Solomon. She's the only person I've seen other than him and his father in what has to be months. I could cry from the relief of it.

"Magna, I—"

"Don't speak to her," Solomon orders sternly. He's got a worried look on his face and I find it uneasy that he's refusing to look at me. Usually, his eye contact is too much.

"How am I supposed to work in these conditions?" The old woman searches the space around us looking unimpressed.

"I could fetch another lantern," Solomon suggests, but she shakes her head firmly.

All the women go to Magna when they're expecting a child, She's delivered all the babies in the village and, although her bedside manner leaves a lot to be desired, I'm glad she's here to check up on mine.

"Here, get her to lie on this plastic sheet." She hands something to Solomon who steps toward me.

"You need to lie on this." He flattens the sheet out on the floor and when Magna starts to wash her hands in the basin in the corner, the guilty look she gives me over her shoulder turns my relief into nerves.

"What is she here for?" I hold my hand over my tummy protectively.

"You're starting to show that little gift I gave you." He reaches out to take my wrist but I quickly pull away. "Father can't know what happens between us. You're not a chosen one, Everleigh." He lowers his head sadly.

"No." I back myself up against the wall.

"Magna won't tell, she owes me a favor." He takes my wrist, dragging me toward the sheet, and I dig my heels into the ground below, trying to stop him. "She's going to fix it, and make sure this never happens to you again." His strength is too great as he wraps me up in his arms and lowers me onto the plastic sheet.

"No, please. Don't... Don't do that." I thrash against him when he sits me between his legs, holding me firm as I kick to get free, and forces my body back against his chest. His hand covers over my mouth and the cloth it's holding blocks all my airways. I lose all my fight, and my body goes limp.

"I wish things could be different," I hear him whisper, and the look of guilt on Magna's face is the last thing I see before everything blurs to darkness.

I don't know how long I was out, but I'm alone when I wake up.

It's pitch black and the pain that stabs through me when I sit up makes me wail. My insides feel as if they've been torn out and stuffed back inside me, and I clutch my stomach knowing that my baby's been taken from me.

"I'm sorry." I hear a voice come from the darkness, and although I can't see him, I know it's Solomon.

"Why? Why did you let me keep it for so long? Why let me grow it inside me?" I sob. My child wasn't conceived out of love, and what I would have delivered it into is nothing but evil, but it was a part of me, one that he allowed me to nurture and fall in love with.

"I liked how you were when you were hopeful. I liked how it felt to go against him," he admits, sounding weak and strained. "If your stupid sister hadn't run away I would have had you, you would have been my wife and I could have given you as many babies as you could carry. But now..." I feel him move closer. "Now you will have none."

"No." I shake my head and cry.

"This is your life now, Everleigh, the black is the only future you have. It will be better this way. You wouldn't have wanted to go through that again, it wasn't pleasant." He strokes my face and when I feel his mouth just a breath away from mine, I clam up.

"Our secret, remember?" He presses his lips softly against mine and I swear I feel one of his tears drip onto my cheek. "Rest, I'll bring you something nice for breakfast tomorrow morning." He stands up and leaves me

I toss the journal at the wall when going back to that place feels too torturous. I don't know if that memory can ever be blocked out. I think about the baby that I never got to meet every day. I think about the others there might have been if Addison hadn't run away, and if Solomon hadn't taken away my ability to be a mother.

I don't blame my sister for escaping, but I *do* blame her for not taking me with her. I blame her for the nights I had to take her husband's cock in my ass. I blame her for Solomon's secrets, and I blame her for the fact I never met my child.

Days like today are hard, I want to scream, I want to go outside and kick down an outhouse like Mitch did, but I saw the way those doctors looked at me back in Colorado after I was saved. They wanted to lock me away, and if it hadn't been for the bikers who were there that day they would have. Being here is a blessing, and I need to start appreciating it.

I leave my journal on the floor and head out the door, taking a big inhale of fresh air as I step off the porch and head across the yard to the outhouse that Mitch is fixing up.

"Ev—" He stops what he's doing as I approach him, staring at me in shock.

"I want you to show me some of this place," I tell him, standing tall and keeping my back straight. I meant what I said earlier this morning about proving myself to him, and I want new, happy memories to help dull out the bad ones.

"You wanna go explorin'?" I get the sense he doesn't quite believe me when he tilts his head sideways and creases his brow.

"You said there were all kinds of wildlife around here, I want you to show me some."

"Well, then, we best get started." He drops the hammer he's holding and moves toward his truck, opening the passenger seat door for me. My stomach starts to tie up in knots, but I smile and get inside anyway. Nothing ventured, nothing gained, that's what Addison always used to tell me. But I don't want to think about her, or where we came from right now. There's a different feeling mixed up with all my nerves, one that I haven't felt since I was a child. I think it might be excitement.

Mitch drives us further away from the cabin, and when I

see a huge ranch coming up in the distance I start to wonder if I've pushed myself too far.

"You're taking me to where you work?" I hear the horror in my voice because I know from what he tells me some nights that the Carson ranch is busy. There's sure to be lots of people there and although I'm feeling adventurous, I'm not ready for that.

"Only to get somethin', we'll be there five minutes. Tops. And ya don't have to speak to anyone ya don't want to," he assures me.

"Everyone's gonna know who I am. I'm the cult girl freak and I don—"

"You're not a freak," he cuts me off sternly. "And ain't no one here's gonna look at ya that way." He pulls up in a very busy yard, and I stay rooted to my seat as he gets out and makes his way into one of the stables.

One of the men who passes the window raises his hat at me and smiles, and I smile back awkwardly as I continue to wait for Mitch, breathing myself calm.

There's so much going on I don't know what to look at first. Being here is a reminder that while I've been locked in a bunker and living inside my head, the world around me has carried on.

Mitch steps out the stable leading his horse, and when he opens up my door I feel my pulse start to quicken.

"I also told ya that the best way to tour the ranch is on horseback." He reminds me, holding out his hand for me to take.

"You want me to ride him?" I look up at his beautiful, but very large, brown horse.

"We're both gonna ride him. You ain't gonna see no wildlife drivin' around in a truck with a loud engine and a rattly exhaust."

I take another leap of faith, gripping his hand and letting him help me out of my seat. I try not to take notice of all the people around us and focus on Mitch.

"Now, put ya foot in this stirrup and I'll help you up," Mitch instructs me, and I jump when I feel his hands lift under me and force me over the saddle. "Sorry, ma'am, there ain't no polite way to do that." He smiles up at me before taking the reins in one hand and lifting himself up behind me.

"Put ya hands here and hold on." He places my hands on the front of the saddle. "Rest back against me, and just go with the rhythm of the horse." He clicks his tongue and I hold my breath, closing my eyes as we start moving forward.

"Open your eyes, darlin'," Mitch whispers in my ear. "You've spent long enough in the dark."

I open them on his command and notice how everyone in the yard has stopped what they're doing to stare at us, and suddenly I feel very exposed.

"What ya'll starin' at? Ain't ya ever seen a cowboy give a lady a ride before? Get back to work," he orders, before kicking us on and making us move a little faster.

I don't know how long we ride for but the thrill of it quickly takes over all the nerves I'd built up. I know I'm safe with Mitch, and now we're out of the yard it's just me and him. I feel so free in all the space surrounding us.

The sky is bright blue and seems to roll on forever, there's nothing but mountains, trees, and pastures for miles. And I like how it feels to have Mitch's arms wrapped around me.

"Sorry, there ain't much about today." He eventually brings us to a stop. "There's a stream just through those trees, we should get JD some water." He slides off the saddle and leads me and his horse toward the tree line. I grip the saddle a little tighter, knowing I haven't got him for stability.

"It's beautiful here, I can see why you've made it your home." When we get to the stream he tethers the horse near the water and helps me down off the saddle. He sits on one of the rocks and I can tell from the way he's frowning that he has something on his mind.

"I never really thought about goin' any place else. This is the only home I've ever had and the only life I've ever wanted." He frowns as he watches the water meander through the rocks in front of us.

"Well, I think it's perfect. It's pretty and it's calm." I take a seat beside him.

"Kinda like you." He turns his head to look at me. "Now, do ya understand why I want you to see the world? There's so much more like this out there."

"No one's ever gonna see the whole world," I laugh, trying my best to lighten his mood. Up to now, I've had the best day of my life, I don't want it to be ruined by him thinking he knows what's best for me. "I think the world is what you make it, and you've made your own little paradise here." I think back to the time when my world was in that bunker. I woke up every day hoping it would be my last. I became numb and unaffected by all the things Abraham did to me. I let myself believe that what he and Solomon did to me was normal. Now I'm away from it all I'm realizing how horrific it all was.

"You should make your own world too." Mitch picks up a stone and throws it into the water. "Meet a guy your age, get married, have some kids."

"I can't have kids," I tell him, picking up a stone myself and launching it at the water. It doesn't go as far as Mitch's but it does make an impressive splash.

"Sure ya can, you're gettin' better every day. I'll bet two weeks ago you would never have seen yourself sitting he—"

"No, I mean, I can't physically... It's one of the things that was done to me back at the village." I close my eyes when I see the horror on his face. It's why I don't speak to people about this stuff, it's just as hard for them to hear as it is for me to say.

"They did *that* to you?" His hand grips at mine and his voice sounds just as shocked as it is angry.

"Unfortunately, they did, so there are no kids in my future. And I guess there'll be no husband either because who wants a wife that can't produce children?"

"Everleigh, you're not in the village anymore. People don't think like that. Plenty of women who can't have kids of their own still become moms. And men don't measure women by how many kids they can give 'em. They get married because they love 'em and because they don't want to spend a single day without 'em by their side. Believe me when I tell ya, Evy, it won't be hard for you to find someone to love ya."

"And what if the person who I want doesn't want me back?" I ask him, wishing I could know what goes on in his head and why he's so determined to deny what this could be.

"Come on, we should get back to the ranch." He stands up and dusts off his jeans, cutting the conversation before it even gets started.

We ride all the way back in silence, and for some of the journey I drop off to sleep with my head resting back against Mitch. That scent of hard work and leather seems to have become a comforter to me and I fear nothing when I'm with him, today is proof of that.

The yard's much quieter when we get back and when Mitch lifts me down from the saddle, I follow him into the stable and smile when I see the horse he brought home with him yesterday.

"Hey, you." I head over to stroke her and she blows in my face like she's happy to see me.

I watch Mitch take the saddle off his horse and get him some water and can't help admiring how good he looks while doing it.

The guys I saw out in the yard earlier may be younger than him, but Mitch seems to have something they don't.

I'm starting to understand why the woman in the book Savannah gave me likes the things her man does to her, so much. When he touches his woman she doesn't flinch, when he puts himself inside her it brings her pleasure not pain, and in one part I read he'd kissed her between her legs purely to make *her* feel good.

"You okay there, darlin'?" Mitch laughs to himself when he catches me daydreaming.

"Yeah... I'm fine." I blush when he interrupts the vision I have in my head of him with his mouth on me.

"You're lookin' a little hot, you want me to get ya some water too?"

"Honestly, I'm fine." I get back to stroking the golden-colored horse and try to ignore the strange pulse that's beating in the pit of my stomach.

I can feel it happening, that thing I spent fifty years avoiding, is coming at me like a ten-ton truck.

Just looking at Everleigh hurts, she's beyond beautiful, she's beyond anything I've ever encountered in my life and the thought of those cult assholes taking something so precious from her makes me murderous.

Everleigh would have been a good mother, she's caring and nurturing. She constantly puts other people's needs before her own, and it's cruel that she'll never have the chance to grow a child of her own inside her body.

She seems determined to prove to me that she belongs here and I wish it was as easy as that. I can't take advantage of the submission that's been embedded into this girl. She needs proper help, and she needs to explore all the other options that are out there for her. I can see her getting better every day, and soon she'll start believing in herself. Until then I'll be the man who she clings to in her sleep, even if I'm setting myself up for heartbreak.

We manage to get out the yard without anyone speaking to us, and once we're back in the truck, I drive toward the cabin, admiring the way she looks out the window as the wind blows through her hair. The thought of a girl as pretty as her being interested in me seems laughable.

I've never struggled to find female company and I've brought many women back to the bunk house, but never have I considered settling down with any of 'em. I've never wanted more than a few hours of their attention, and I've certainly never been good at giving them any of mine.

With Everleigh it's different, I could spend hours just looking at her. Every little thing she does fascinates me, even the way she's started chewing on her hair when she's reading one of Savannah's books. I love the way whatever it is she's reading makes her blush. I love the way her hands feel when they touch me, and I love the idea of the man I want to be for her. There's no denying what this is now, I've watched many men fall victim to it. Now I understand why Garrett never lets Maisie out of his sight, and why Wade went off the rails after Leia married that sick little Mason bastard. I get why Cole lost a part of himself when Aubrey died and how he found it again in Savannah, but that doesn't make our stories the same. I can't let myself drown in this, because there will come a time when I have to let her go.

I spend what's left of the afternoon making the outhouse suitable to stable, both JD and the horse I'm bringing back here for Everleigh. This place has become my home now and it seems stupid not to have my horse with me. I like the flexibility of having JD close. What's the use of a cowboy without his horse?

Everleigh sits out on the porch reading her book and every time I glance over my shoulder and catch her watching me, she gets that same embarrassed look on her face that makes me wonder what the hell she's reading about.

It's baking hot so I have my shirt off, and the way her eyes keep looking over me feels kinda exposing. I like it, it makes me feel a lot less guilty about the way I look at her.

When I decide I'm done for the day I lift my shirt from the fence post, slinging it over my shoulder as I walk toward the cabin. When Everleigh sees me coming she immediately places down her book and stands up.

"You done?" she asks, almost seeming as skittish as that damn horse I just bought for her.

"For today. I'm gonna need more timber to get it finished. I can grab some tomorrow."

"You look hot, do you want a glass of muscle... I mean water?" She shakes her head and looks up from my chest with fast-beating lashes and rosy cheeks.

"I'm good, I was just about to grab a shower." I glance down to the book she's reading and she quickly turns it over so I don't see the half-naked guy on the front of it.

"I'll just get back to my book." She's clearly trying to hide something from me and she looks fuckin' adorable while doing it.

"Everleigh..." I wait until she's sitting back down and when she looks at me with that smile still on her face, another chunk of my heart gives itself away. "Thank you for today. For sharin' with me what happened to ya, I know it can't have been easy."

"It was easier than I thought it would be," she admits, waiting for me to leave her before she buries her head back into the pages.

It takes some persuasion but Everleigh eventually allows me to take care of the cooking tonight, and watching her reaction to her first-ever corn dog was as hilarious as it was cute. I'm still smiling from it when we settle down in the living room and although her nose is still buried in that goddamn book, I can feel her eyes glance at me as I strum my guitar and hum to myself.

"Is it okay if I take a shower?" she asks, and I hate that after all this time she still feels as if she needs my permission.

"Of course." I smile over at her, noticing that she places her book pages down on the couch before she gets up and heads for the bathroom. I let curiosity get the better of me when I immediately get up and reach for it. I make sure I keep one finger on the page she's on as I flick back through what she's been reading today.

My eyes widen at the words that are in front of me, the same words that have kept Everleigh so intrigued. Hell, even some of the bunkhouse boys would blush from the words that I'm reading.

Now that I got a sense of what's been keeping her so entertained, I quickly set the book back down exactly how I found it and retake my chair. I have to try my best to unsee the words I've just read because keeping my cock down around Everleigh is a hard enough task as it is.

She smiles at me shyly when she comes out the bathroom wearing just a towel, and as she scurries through to the bedroom to put on her nightdress my eyes glance back over to the book. I need to cool myself off, so I head outside to take a smoke.

He comes to bed about an hour after I turn in, soothing all that worry I've built up that he wouldn't. I've felt us get closer today. I dropped my guard a little more and I still can't believe how much I opened up to him down by the stream. I don't even regret it. How could I when he was so kind and understanding about it all?

Mitch nods his head at me, looking almost shy when he steps into the room and slides out of his jeans. He keeps on his tee and boxers like he did last time he joined me in bed, and when he gets under the covers he lies back as if he's not entirely sure how to position himself. I lean over and press and kiss on his cheek before turning my back on him and snuggling into my pillow.

"Good night, Mitch." I close my eyes and try to picture the look on his face. I know that it's important that I take things slow, but venturing away from the cabin isn't the only thing I'd like to try. I want to know how it feels to have Mitch touch me, and not just on the cheek or my hand. In a much more intimate way. The same way that the guy in my book touches his girl. I've even been wondering since this morning what his mouth would feel like exploring me all over and when I do, I get that pulsing in my stomach again.

"Good night, darlin'." His low, raspy voice and the comfort of knowing he's close makes me smile to myself, and we both lie in complete silence for what feels like hours.

I can sense he's still awake, and I will for him to put his arms around me the way he did when we were riding earlier.

"You know, you don't need to ask permission or wait till I'm asleep before you touch me." I close my eyes in shame as I force the words out my mouth.

Mitch doesn't answer straight away, but after a few seconds, I feel his hand slide over my hip and cross over my stomach. The bed creaks as he shifts his body closer to mine, ensuring my back is against his chest the way it was earlier. I feel my whole body relax from the comfort of it.

"It's different with you, Mitch. I don't fear your touch, I don't fear anything about you at all." I reach my hand back to stroke over his leg.

"I'd be careful doin' that, sweetheart," he warns me, but I don't listen. I want to experience intimacy with this man. I want to push my boundaries. And that's exactly what happens when I feel something hard press against my lower back.

"That's what I was warnin' ya 'bout." Mitch looks embarrassed when I glance over my shoulder at him. "I'm sorry. I'll just step outside for a while, it'll go away." He goes to move but I shake my head.

"No." I turn so I'm facing him. "Maybe I could make it go away for you?" I suggest, watching his eyes widen in shock.

"I think you're the one who's causin' the problem, darlin'." He smirks at me, and I wipe it right off his face when I slide my hand into the waistband of his boxers and wrap it around his manhood.

"*Holy shit!*" He looks between us in even more shock as my

fingers start to stroke over his thick, solid cock the same way I read about earlier.

"Ev—I—"

"I want to do this for you." I hold eye contact so he knows I mean it. Nothing about this is the same as before, I feel completely in control and it's incredible.

"Baby, this is gonna complicate things." He shakes his head while his tongue rolls inside his cheek.

"You've never called me that before." I frown back at him as my hand keeps its steady rhythm.

"Well, with all respect, you ain't never had your hand wrapped around my cock before either." He smiles.

"And do you like how it feels?" Mitch's cock feels so much bigger than what I've been used to, it's thick and very heavy, but I don't let that intimidate me.

"It feels *real* good, darlin'." He places his hand on the back of my head as he keeps his eyes focused between us. "I wanna watch," he whispers. "I wanna see your hand workin' me. I'll bet it looks as good as it feels too."

I nod my head as he sets to work, pulling back the covers and slipping his boxers off his hips. Now that I see him for the first time I understand why it felt so different. Mitch's manhood is enormous and as he watches my hand slide over it, I feel his grip on my hair tighten and his body go tense.

"That feels so fuckin' good," he growls at me, looking like he's on the verge of losing control, and then he does something that takes me completely by surprise.

His hand slides behind my ear and he draws my face closer to his so he can kiss me with lips that are much softer than I've imagined them to be. The way they move against mine is urgent, demanding and seems to match the desperation that's building up inside me.

"Fuck, Ev. That's so good," he pulls back to tell me, and

knowing that I'm causing him so much pleasure lights a fire up inside me. I need his lips on me again so I lean back into him and take them.

"Darlin', I'm gonna come, you gotta stop." Mitch takes hold of my wrist in his hand and tries to tug me away, but I'm not finished. I want Mitch to spill his seed and I don't care if it's onto my hand. I don't even care if he puts it in my mouth, in fact, I'm curious about how he tastes. So curious that I lower my head and slip my lips over the head of his thickness. He gasps in shock and grips my hair in his fist. "*Holy fuck, Everleigh!*" His words come out strained. There's no way I can take all of him in my mouth, not without choking, so I keep my hand moving and just focus on his tip.

"I'm comin'," he growls another warning, before tensing his fingers and filling my mouth with spurts of warm, sticky pleasure that I've caused. I swallow him down while looking up at him and watch as confusion takes over the tension on his handsome face.

"I wanted to taste you." I shrug, suddenly hoping I haven't overstepped the mark and got him mad at me.

"Get up here," he orders me with narrow eyes and a stern look on his face. Taking my chin between his thumb and finger he guides me to climb back up the bed toward him. Our eyes stay in contact and I let go of the breath I've been holding when he kisses me again, his fingers gripping me tight while his lips touch me softly.

"Well, ain't you full of surprises?" He smiles as he shakes his head in shock, and when I wrap my arms around his muscular torso and rest my head on his chest, I allow myself to slip into a deep, contented sleep.

CHAPTER 17

MITCH

"We need to talk about the books that your wife has been recommendin' to Everleigh." I storm into Cole's cabin without knocking.

"Mornin', Mitch." He lifts his hat from the table and places it on his head before he stands.

"Is she here?" I check around us for any signs of Savannah.

"You just missed her, she left to go shoppin' with Leia."

"Do you know what kinda things are in those books, they're—"

"I know what's in 'em. Some of my wife's best ideas come outta those books," he interrupts me with a grin on his face.

"Well, I don't know if it's the kinda thing Everleigh should be readin'. I think they might be givin' her ideas too. She keeps on lookin' at me weird and last night..." I manage to stop myself before I overshare, but when one of his eyebrows rises, I know I've already given too much away.

"It's wrong, a girl her age, after all she's been through." I press my fingers into the table and focus on them rather than facing his judgment.

"You think it's wrong for her to explore how it's supposed to be between a man and a woman?" He laughs at me.

"Of course, I don't, I just think it's wrong that she's doin' it with me." I grow the balls to look back up at him. "She... She had her hand on my damn cock, Cole. I ain't a fuckin' saint." I scrub my hand over my face because for all of my sins, what I let happen last night feels like the worst of 'em.

"Has it occurred to you how much confidence that would have taken her to do? Jimmer explained to us all what she's been through, and I'm guessin' we only know half of it. She's been here for six months, and you and that cabin is all she's known."

"Which is exactly my point. She's clearly ready to heal, and she's thinkin' I'm her only option. I'm her safe zone, and if I let this go on I'll be doin' her more harm than good." Hearing the words out loud only makes me feel more guilty about what I'm allowing to happen.

"Ever thought that maybe she's just fallen for the kind, considerate man who's been takin' care of her all this time?" Cole frowns at me. "C'mon, Mitch. We've all noticed a change in ya, and it ain't just because Dalton's gone. Ya can't deny that you look forward to goin' home to her, and I can guarantee that it's her who's on your mind most of the day while you're workin'." He may hit the nail in straight but it makes no difference to the situation.

"That's not what matters here, that girl needs help. Jimmer saved her from those cult bastards, now I need to save her from herself." That sting finds its way to my chest again when I think about having to distance myself from her. Especially when I know that Cole is right, what happened between us last night was some real progress for her. The fact she trusted me to be the one she made that progress means the fuckin' world to me. The last thing I want to do is throw that back at her.

"Mitch, this girl likes you, she's got a therapist, and—"

"She's young enough to be my daughter. What the hell

does a girl her age want with a grumpy, old cowboy?" I laugh bitterly.

"She's not like other girls. She's been through hell and she sees this world differently to others. In normal circumstances the two of you would probably never have met. But ya have, and you've been showin' her that side to ya that ya only ever let the people close to ya see. I don't think your age is a problem here. I don't think she is either. I think *you* are too scared to fall in love." He crosses his arms and stares at me with a smart look on his face.

"Me, in love?" I snort. "Cole, I've made it this far in my life without bein' a victim to that."

"Being in love don't make ya a victim." Now it's his turn to laugh. "Sure, it makes ya vulnerable and I know from experience that it can fuckin' hurt, but there comes a time when you can't protect yourself from it. It takes over your head and all your senses. Then overrules all your doubts and good intentions. The books ain't what made Everleigh wanna touch ya last night. *You* did."

I scratch the back of my neck and stare back at him, wondering to myself how the hell Cole Carson suddenly became the voice of reason.

"Look, Savannah's been goin' on about includin' the girl in more stuff, around here. She likes her, and ya know what she gets like when she's got her mind set on somethin'."

"I don't, Cole, I don't wanna push her."

"I was gonna suggest we have Savannah take over from Josie for a while. I figure if she's at your place bein' *useful*, she won't be able to help out at the guesthouse anymore. I really need her to start slowin' down."

"I think Everleigh would like that." I nod in agreement. I've seen a change in her since she started speaking to Savannah, and although the girl can be a lot to handle, her enthusiasm is kinda infectious. Maybe she's just what Everleigh needs.

"I'll have her come by tomorrow then." Cole leads me to the door.

"That new kid, he's dedicated," he mentions as I untether JD and lead him over toward the stable where Cole keeps Rebel.

"Yeah, I've been hearing' good things about him." I pass Cole his saddle while he dusts off Rebel's back.

"Garrett tells me the kids up with the sun ridin' that horse you bought from Wade. She's still a little jumpy but even Wade's impressed with the improvement."

"Maybe she just needed some time and consistency. Wade's got a lot on, with the baby and all." I shrug.

"He sure does." Cole blows out a breath as he checks the strap is tight around Rebel's belly then jumps on his saddle

"You gettin' nervous?" I ask, knowing that before Savannah, having kids would never have been a thought in his head.

"I don't think there's a man who's about to become a father that ain't. I just hope my best is good enough." He shrugs.

"You know it will be." I hop up on JD so we can ride to the ranch together.

"Who knows, maybe you might find out yourself some day?" Cole raises his eyebrows at me for the second time today.

"Nah, Everleigh can't have kids anyway." I shake my head.

"Now who said that I was suggestin' you have 'em with her?" The clever bastard winks at me as he kicks Rebel into a gallop and leaves me with something to think about.

We arrive at the ranch within five minutes, all the Carson brothers' homes are close, mainly because their women are so close and it means they don't have to stray too far to be together. The girls are all so kind and supportive of each other.

It's the sorta thing Everleigh should experience after all she's been through.

"Hey, Mitch." Maisie steps out onto the porch with one of the triplets resting on her hip, and I smile at the little fella before I pretend to pull off his nose.

"Have you seen what Hunter's managed to do?" She nods her head over to the corral where Hunter has the skittish horse that Everleigh has fallen in love with trotting around it at a steady pace. "Garrett says he's put in hours of work, all in his own time. He's impressed."

"Yeah, well, he seems like a good kid." I watch him as he continues to ride, wondering who he is and where he came from. He's taken to the saddle like a duck to water, and he's proving that he's eager to impress. You don't get many kids like that these days.

"He's the kind of help we could do with." Cole lifts his nephew up outta Maisie's arms and sits him on the front of his saddle.

"You're as bad as Garrett. Let's get him walking first, huh?" She reaches up to take him back, but the kid proves he's a true Carson when he grips the reins and turns his head away from her.

"Maybe in a few years, champ." Cole laughs to himself as he hands him back down. "Garrett workin' in his office today?" he asks, looking around the yard and seeing no sign of him.

"He's on mayor duties, and not the slightest bit happy about it." Maisie rolls her eyes.

"Well, he made Harvey a promise, and this town's gonna be a better place with him in charge," Cole reminds her, proving again how much he's changed. He used to hate the world, now he seems determined to find the best in it.

"He's worried about Bianca Mason, I can tell." She lowers her voice.

"Yeah, well, he ain't got no need for that, we took care of the last Mason problem just fine," Cole sniggers and Maisie narrows her eyes like she's about to scold him.

"I don't think you can handle Bianca in quite the same way." She reminds him of the fact the last Mason problem ended up with two deaths to cover up.

"I think I've proven that, if I have to, I will. Whatever it takes." Cole nods his head before moving on.

"You don't think he would—"

"Maisie, darlin', when it comes to this family I wouldn't rule out anythin'." I move along with him, nodding my head at Hunter and letting him see that I'm impressed.

CHAPTER 18

EVERLEIGH

I practically pace the floor waiting for Mitch to come home. I fell into such a deep sleep last night that I never woke up until he'd left for work. In fact, Josie was already here when I got my lazy ass out of bed.

I've spent the entire day wondering if things will be different between us now. I know I was forward last night, and I can't imagine what Mitch must be thinking, but at the same time, I really liked how it felt to be in control.

I touched him on my own terms and it gave him pleasure, pleasure that felt like such a reward.

He can't have been too mad, because he kissed me after, and I swear I've felt the touch of it on my lips ever since.

The fact he left without saying goodbye this morning has me scared that he'll come home tonight and try to push me away the same way he did before.

"Well, I'm outta here. I have a date tonight." Josie jumps up from the couch as soon as the clock strikes five-thirty.

"Okay." I smile back at her guiltily, I haven't been good company today, not that I'm much on any other day. But I can feel everything changing. I have the drive and determination to get better. To be confident and to have more experiences with Mitch like I did last night.

I wait until Josie has left before I pick up my book and head out to sit on the porch. The open space I look out onto doesn't seem half as scary now that I've explored it with Mitch, and when I eventually see him riding toward me in the distance, I stand up and wait for him to get closer.

He looks so handsome when he's riding. To be honest, he looks handsome doing pretty much anything, and when he jumps off his saddle and ties his horse to the railings, I'm a little taken aback when he suddenly grabs hold of my hips and steers my body to align with his.

"I'm sorry that I left this morin' without sayin' goodbye. My head was a mess." He shakes his head as if his own words are confusing him.

"I hate that you've been through hell, I wish I could go back in time and make it all go away. I wish I was the man who'd killed whoever treated you so bad and did those terrible things to you. But I *like* that I'm your comfort now. I *love* that you trust me, and although I feel like I don't deserve it, that don't mean I won't treasure it. Shit, I'm rantin' and all my words are comin' out wrong." He stops to take a breath, and when a tiny smile lifts his lips my whole chest fills with warmth.

"Everleigh, I like you very much. I spend my whole day wonderin' what you're doin' and lookin' forward to seein' ya. I'm too old for ya, and you may not even be seein' me in the same way that I see you, but this is me promisin' never to run scared on you again."

"You were scared?" I whisper, still shocked at what I'm hearing. I can't imagine Mitch being scared of anything, especially me.

"Yes, I'm scared. I'm scared of how you make me feel. I'm scared that I ain't enough, but most of all I'm scared of hurtin' ya. You looked so peaceful while you were sleepin' last night. And ya keep sayin' that I'm a good man and I'm sorry to tell ya, darlin', but that ain't always the case. I've done things that I'm probably goin' to Hell for, but you need to know that I would never do anythin' to hurt ya."

His hand reaches up to cradle my face and his thumb strokes my cheek.

"I know things are gonna be hard and if all you ever want me to be is the man who holds you at night, then I'll be grateful for it." His deep scratchy voice makes my stomach flip.

"I don't just want that. I like the way it feels when you touch me. I liked the way you kissed me." I feel my cheeks heat up when I think about all the other things I've imagined us doing. "I just wish I could be normal and—"

"Sweetheart, we don't do normal around here, we are who we are and everyone accepts that. You just have to learn to be okay with yourself." His lips are so temptingly close that I crave them even more.

"Mitch," I whisper his name.

"Yeah, darlin'?"

"I'd very much like it if you kissed me again." I smile up at him, feeling that same spark of thrill as I did when I took him in my hand last night.

"I'd very much like that too." He takes off his hat and leans closer, connecting his lips to mine and making that flutter in my stomach turn into something much stronger. I gasp out loud when he suddenly lifts me off my feet.

"What are you doing?" I ask, clinging to his arms as he places my ass down on the porch rail.

"I'm just making sure you're comfortable because I plan on kissin' ya for a really long time." He places his hat on top of my head and gets back to it.

We spend a long time with our lips locked together and our tongues exploring. I love the way his hands feel as they stroke my face and glide down my spine. It makes me want to give him so much more of myself. I just don't want to bear the shame of taking off my clothes in front of him. My past has left me with scars. Deep, ugly ones that I can't even look at myself. The thought of Mitch seeing them forces me to be the first of us to pull away.

"I should make you some dinner." I smile apologetically, rubbing my lips together and liking the way they taste of him now.

"And I should get JD down for the night." Mitch nods his head toward his horse who's been standing very patiently. He kisses me one last time before he takes his reins and leads him over to the stable he's been working on. I stand and watch him with my fingers pressed against my lips and when he looks back over his shoulder at me, I shamelessly stare and allow that giddy happiness I'm feeling to find its way to my lips.

I rustle up something fast because when Mitch comes back inside all I want to do is kiss him again. I make us some grilled cheese and we both smile at each other over the table as we eat it. There's a different kind of comfort between us now, one more intense than the one that was there before, and when Mitch reaches his hand across the table to hold mine while he continues to eat, I feel myself fall even harder for him.

All the things he said earlier gave me such hope, and only makes me more determined to get myself better.

"I was talkin' to Cole today," he informs me once we're finished.

"Savannah's husband?" I check.

"That's the one, he was sayin' that Savannah wants to include you in—"

"Yes," I cut him off before he's even finished his sentence. I don't care what it is, if it's a chance for me to move forward I'll take it. I don't want to be a prisoner in my own head anymore. Not when I could be making happy memories with Mitch. Ever since that night, I fell asleep on the couch in his arms, I don't feel scared by the world. I'm intrigued by it.

"We thought we'd start by havin' her come here, instead of Josie. You can go at your own pace with the other girls, and they're all keen to meet ya," he assures me.

"And do we keep this a secret?" I look down at where our hands are still touching.

"You can tell them whatever ya want. Around here nothin' stays secret for long anyway." He chuckles to himself as he stands up and picks up our plates. I watch him run the faucet after he's put them in the sink and quickly get up to take over.

"You ain't doin' this tonight." He shocks me when he lifts me up again and settles me on the kitchen work surface.

"Why not?" I giggle.

"Because I want ya to sit there and look pretty while I do it." He kisses my cheek before getting to work and as I watch him soap up the dishes, I smile to myself.

"I'm gonna be okay." The words inside my head just float out of my mouth and I feel the freedom in them as well as the relief.

"'Course, ya are." Mitch frowns at me, drying off his hands and moving to position himself between the gap in my legs. "I don't think you realize how far you've come. You're not that silent girl who I first saw in Jimmer Carson's basement anymore." His eyes move over my body with desire as well as pride.

"I feel less and less like her every day," I admit as I touch my palms over his chest. "I want to get better for you, Mitch. And you're wrong when you say you're too old for me. Where I came from husbands wer—"

"We ain't where you came from no more, Evy. There are people out there that will be ready to judge us, but I don't care about them, not so long as you're happy." He furrows his brow as if he needs to hear me say it.

"Well, I am happy. Really happy." I wrap my arms around his neck and kiss him again.

"So, what's this all about?" Tate looks around the stable where I've gathered everyone together. Garrett looks concerned as he props his shoulder against one of the pillars, while Cole rests back against one of the paddock doors like he's got a good guess at what's coming.

"I just thought I'd get ya all together to bring ya up to speed. Most of ya know that for some time I've been livin' in the cabin up on Grid 3 with a young woman who's been through some tough times." I swallow thickly when I notice the look that Wade and Finn give each other.

"Well, me and that woman. We have... erm... Well, we've... We're together now... I think." I hate how my words are coming out so weak and unsure.

"That's what you called us all here to announce?" Wade laughs.

"Well, you know me and how I feel about whispers."

"Mitch, I think we all knew about you and that girl before you did." Finn takes his hat off his head so he can run his fingers through his thick brown hair.

"I...What... How?" I shake my head in disbelief.

"That girl's changed ya. We've all been seein' it," he informs me. "It's about time you owned it."

"Well, then, I guess you can all get back to work." I gesture my head to the door, and once they've all dispersed, Garrett pushes himself off the pillar to make his way over.

"This is good to hear. It's about time you focused on somethin' other than this place." He slaps my arm.

"I feel outta my depth. Way outta it," I admit, shaking my head at him. I spent most of last night watching Everleigh sleeping. Before that, we spent the whole night just kissin' on the couch. It felt like the most intimate thing I'd ever done. I can feel myself getting swept away in all the goodness she expels, and I can't lose sight of all the real-life things we have to face.

"It's scary, but it'll be worth it," Garrett assures me. "You need this, Mitch. For years you've been tellin' me and my brothers to trust our instincts and follow our hearts, now's the time to be takin' your own advice." He grips my shoulder and smiles.

"She's gettin' better every day and as beautiful as it is to watch, I got no experience in how to handle these kindsa things. I've never had a woman of my own. I don't wanna let her down," I admit, hating how helpless I feel.

"Mitch, you ain't gonna let her down, you're the most reliable guy I've ever met. You managed to raise half-decent men outta us three, so you can do anythin' ya put your mind to. Any woman who's loved by you is a lucky one."

We both turn our heads when the stable door slams and when it rebounds off the hinge and opens back up again, it's Hunter we see storming across the yard toward the bunkhouse.

"What the hell was that all about?" Garrett frowns as he watches him disappear inside and slam another door behind him.

"I don't know, but I'm findin' out." I quickly march across the yard to go after him and when I fling open the door and see Hunter pulling his holdall from under his bunk, I stand back and watch in confusion.

"Plannin' on goin' somewhere?" I ask, folding my arms and keeping calm.

"Looks that way, don't it?" He keeps his eyes focused on the clothes that he's packing.

"What's gotten into you, boy?" I step closer and when he turns to face me I see the pure, aggravated rage on his face.

"I came here wanting to impress you. I wanted to prove that I can do this."

"And ya have. Everyone out there is singin' ya praises," I point out, still confused as to what all this is about.

"I thought you'd be the one teachin' me. I thought..." He silences himself then shakes his head and continues to stuff all his possessions in his bag.

"What are ya talkin' about, kid? Look, I don't know what's got ya so triggered but—"

"I'm wondering if my mother was one of those *lucky* girls who got to be loved by you?" He stops what he's doing and stares at me blankly.

"You're what, now?" I stare hard, trying to understand what I'm hearin'.

"Did she mean *anything* to you?" He stands a little taller and steps toward me. "Do you even remember her name?" The smirk on his face looks as if it comes from disgust.

"Hunter, I don't even know who the hell you're talkin' about." Now *I'm* the one starting to get mad because nothing this boy is saying is making any sense.

"I'm talking about the woman who you knocked up twenty-five years ago." He pulls a piece of paper out from his bedside drawer and shoves it into my chest. Watching me with narrow eyes as I open it up. It's a birth certificate. A birth certificate that has my name written beside the word 'Father'.

"Hunter... I..." I read it over again to be sure.

"Were you the reason she put me up for adoption?" he asks. "Were you not ready to settle down and be a man, then?"

"Hunter... I had no idea about this." I study the mother's name, trying to recall her. I'm ashamed to say over the years there's been more than a few women who have encountered the Mitch Hudson charm, but I've always been careful, and never have I heard from any of 'em that I'd become a father.

"You're trying to tell me you didn't know about this?" Hunter laughs as he snatches it back off me.

"That's *exactly* what I'm tellin' ya, son." I grit my teeth together because this is getting more and more confusing by the second.

"Don't fuckin' call me that!" He points his finger at me warningly, and seeing that his eyes are full of tears is the only thing that holds me back from teaching him a lesson on it.

"You can't just put a random name on a birth certificate, I looked into it. If the parents of the kid ain't married the father either has to be there or sign some consent form," he informs me, looking unconvinced by my defense.

"Well, I can assure you that I didn't sign or agree to anythin'. You must have the wrong Mitch Hudson." I shake my head.

"I don't think so." He delves back into the drawer and pulls out a photo. It's old and a little worn, but it's undeniably me, and the girl I have my arm wrapped around, I do happen to remember.

"That's Naomi Hollins?" My head starts spinning. It's been a long time since I've seen her face.

"My mother." He snatches it back off me and looks down at it fondly.

"Well, you better get hold of your mother and tell her I want to talk to her." I shake my head and try to cast my mind back to a time that seems so long ago.

Naomi was the daughter of the preacher of Fork River back when that photo was taken, and I recall her having a wild streak. There were a few nights where she'd ended up back at the bunkhouse with me, but even in my youth I always played it safe.

"I would if I could, but I can't find her." Hunter stares back at me with all the anger in his eyes broken down to sadness. "I've been looking since I was twenty-one. I managed to track down her family, but the only person still living was her sister. I visited her, showed her the birth certificate and she remembered you from when they lived here," he explains.

"She was the one who gave me the photo." He looks down at it again, as if it's his most treasured possession.

"And this sister, does she know where Naomi is now?" I take a seat on the bunk beside him, trying to find some resemblance between us.

"She didn't even know her sister had had a baby, told me her folks sent Mom away pretty much as soon as they left this town. They moved on to her father's next parish without her. I'm guessing that was because of the trouble she was in. Being knocked up ain't exactly a good look for a preacher's daughter." Hunter shrugs sadly.

"She wasn't a little girl, Hunter, she was a woman." I shake my head and stare at the picture in his hands. Naomi was a fun girl. Pretty too. She knew me well enough to know that if she'd come to me and told me she was in trouble, I'd have helped her.

"No, she wasn't, she was barely seventeen." He defends her again.

"What?" I stand back up in horror. "No, there's no way. I

met her in a bar outta town and gave her a ride home. She told me she'd graduated college."

"Well, then she lied to you because I spoke to her sister and she told me she hadn't even graduated high school."

I slump back down onto his cot feeling sick to my stomach.

"How could you not know her age, she was the preacher's daughter?" he questions me.

"And do I look like the kinda man who goes to church?" I yell back at him, wanting to tear my hair out. "Back then I worked hard and played hard. The only places I ever went beyond this ranch were bars. I swear she told me she was a college graduate." She may have lied to me, but I still can't help feeling sorry for the girl. She must have been so scared. No wonder she didn't come to me for help.

"Why didn't ya tell me this as soon as ya got here?" It suddenly dawns on me that this kid has been here for a whole week.

"I wanted to suss you out first, and maybe I was a little scared of rejection. It ain't every day a guy shows up and tells a man he's his son. I assumed since your name was listed that you'd always known about me."

"Well, I can promise ya that I didn't. If I had...Well, I don't know what I'da done, to be honest, but we sure as hell wouldn't have been meetin' like this." I let it sink in that, for twenty-five years, I've had a kid out in the world that I've played no part in raising.

"We'll have to do tests or somethin' just to be sure, and I understand if now that you know who I am you don't want me workin' here, but—"

"What? Why would I not want ya here?" I look back at him as if he's crazy. "Hunter, all this has come as a shock. A fuckin' huge one. But that don't mean I don't wanna to get to know ya. If all this is right and you are my son, you're exactly where you're supposed to be now." I see the relief on his face when his lips lift into a smile. "I think we need to up our game on findin' your mother. I sure want some answers, and I know someone who can help." I immediately take out my cell and call Jessie, back in Manitou Springs.

"Mitch, it's good to hear from ya. Is everythin' okay with Everleigh?" he asks.

"Everythin's fine, great in fact." I move on from that subject because I'm not gonna go into details on just how good it really is. "I was wonderin' if ya could get your old lady workin' on findin' someone for me."

"Sure, she can, she'll just need a name and whatever you already know," he informs me.

"Appreciated, I'll get a text sent to ya so she can get to work. And, Jess, you know we're here, right? If you need anythin'." I know things back in Colorado must be tough right now. I want Jessie to know that he has our full support.

"I appreciate that too, you just keep takin' care of Addison's sister, she's eager to be reunited with her."

I feel a twist in my gut as I hang up and look back to the kid who's claiming to be my son. I wonder if deep in my subconscious, I knew that he was mine the first moment I set eyes on him. My instincts had instantly told me to trust him, and that ain't something that happens often.

"Maddy's on it, and she's good at what she does," I assure him, hoping that she doesn't take too long in doin' it.

"So, your life before you started lookin'..." I gesture my head toward the piece of paper that says this kid belongs to me. "Was it kind to ya?"

"It was great." He nods his head. "The couple who raised me always made me aware of the fact I was adopted. When I reached twenty-one they gave me all the information they had which was this, and they said it was my choice what I did with it. I'll be honest, at first I wasn't interested. I wanted to focus on the people who wanted to raise me rather than the ones who didn't." He twists up his mouth awkwardly.

"I get that." I nod my head, understanding his logic. "So, what changed your mind?"

"Some girl I went to high school with got herself into the same kinda trouble as my mom did. She decided to do the same and put her baby up for adoption. Speaking to her put some things into perspective for me. People get themselves into all kinds of situations. She knew she wasn't the best option for the baby she was having, but she still wanted him or her to have a good life with everything it needed. I guess I wanted to know if that's how my mom felt about me."

"Listen, kid. I didn't know your mom all too well, but I got the impression she was a good person. She would have wanted you to have everythin'." I think back to the Naomi I vaguely knew. I remember her smiling, and making people laugh.

"We'll find her," I assure him, standing back up. "In the meantime, you just keep doin' what you're doin'. We'll look into gettin' them tests done, and until we know for sure we'll keep this to ourselves."

Hunter nods back in agreement.

"You should have told me." I point my finger at him. "Take that as your lesson of the day. Never, ever assume. Ya ask anyone around here who knows me, I don't shy away from responsibility. I took my nephew in when he was just a kid. If I'da known I had a kid of my own out there things would've been different for you."

I can sense by the way he half smiles back at me that he trusts in what I'm telling him.

"I gotta get back and check on Everleigh, she had a therapy session today. You know where I am if ya need me."

"I'll keep workin' on that mare," he assures me, standing up himself and starting to unpack his clothes.

"Keep up the good work, son." I tap him on the back before walking back out the door. Once I'm out in the fresh air, I'm surprised to find the yard still running the same as it was before he dropped the huge grenade on me. I take a few minutes to get my head around all the information I've just been given.

"The kid okay?" Garrett asks as he rides past me toward the gate.

"Yeah, he's fine." I shrug it off because I'm not ready to share the fact I could have a son who I've let down his entire life just yet.

"Good, hard workers like him are hard to find. They don't make 'em like that anymore." He digs his heels into Thunder's belly and takes off, while I head for the stable to get JD so I can go home.

S amatha left an hour ago, and she seemed impressed with my progress. I told her about my journal entries, and I told her about Savannah. What I didn't tell her about was how much closer I've gotten to Mitch. I'm sure she would believe that what I feel for him is some kind of side effect of my trauma, but I know that it's deeper than that.

Being around Mitch reminds me of the first time Addison told me a fairytale. Those kinds of books were banned from our village, but her best friend Charlie always seemed to find a way of getting us treats from the outside. She kept the fairytale book under a floorboard in our room, and late some nights when we were sure our parents were sleeping, she'd read me the stories in her softest whisper. Stories that always ended so perfectly, with love and happily ever afters. But the beasts didn't turn into princes where we came from. There was no happiness or love, just punishment and control. Mitch gives me that warmth in my heart and the thrill of hope that I'd always feel after hearing one of those stories. I really believe we could have a happy ever after here, in this simple cabin with each other's company.

He comes home earlier than I expected and when he walks

through the door, I instantly sense that he has something on his mind.

"How was your session?" He hangs up his hat and slides his hand through his gray hair.

"It was good, Samantha seemed happy with me." I want to go to him, wrap my arms around his waist, and rest my head on his shoulder, but something in the way he's holding himself is keeping me distanced.

"That's good to hear." He smiles, and although his voice is soothing, I can tell he's not fully here with me.

"And your day?" I ask, hoping that whatever burden he carries he will share. I may be working through my issues but I want to be the person he can talk to when he's had a bad day.

"Darlin', you wouldn't believe me if I told ya." He shakes his head and takes a seat at the table, spacing out and staring at its wood surface.

"Try me." I sit beside him and take his hand in mine.

"I took on a kid at the ranch about a week ago. Hard worker, nice guy," he starts off, then closes his eyes and takes a deep breath. "I found out today that that kid could very well be my son." He opens them back up again and waits for my reaction.

"A son?" It takes me completely off guard, so I can't imagine how he must be feeling.

"Hunter was adopted at birth, his mother never told me about him, but somehow managed to get my name on his birth certificate. He came here lookin' for me and I don't know what he was expectin' to find, but I feel like I've let him down."

"I doubt that. Savannah tells me that all the Carsons and the bunkhouse boys look up to you." I squeeze his hand a little tighter, and he stares at it and shakes his head.

"All those years I was here, tryin' to make decent men outta the Carson brothers, then Dalton. I used to wonder how their own father could have been so useless. And all that time I had my own flesh and blood out there being raised by another man."

"It's not your fault." I can tell how devastated he is and wish there was a way I could make him feel better.

"The whole ride back here, I've thought about all the things I've missed out on. I never got serious enough with anyone to become a father, but I always imagined I'd be kinda good at it. I'm proud every day when I see how far those Carson men have come, and I take a lotta honor in bein' a small part of it. I should be feelin' that about my own boy." He hangs his head and I instantly get up and place myself on his lap.

"You didn't know, Mitch. None of this is your fault. But Hunter's here now, and you have all those opportunities to be his father." My eyes well with tears when I imagine how it would feel to have that opportunity for myself. Then my sadness turns to hate when I think about the man who took that from me.

"I'm sorry, I shouldn't be troublin' ya with this. Ignore me, I'll make us somethin' to eat."

"I was actually thinking that maybe we could go somewhere?" I chew on my nail and wait for his reaction.

"You wanna eat out?" He looks stunned.

"Not exactly, Savannah was telling me that you have a fast food place about an hour from here. She said you can drive around to a window and they pass your food right through to you. Is that true?" I laugh, still unsure if she was teasing me and if I'm making a fool of myself.

"It's true." Mitch smiles for the first time since he's been home.

"Well, she says I haven't lived until I've tried one of their cheeseburgers, and I'm figuring that could be the next step I take. Eating out without having to be inside the restaurant." I look up at him hopefully.

"Ya sure you're ready?" He slides his finger over my cheek to tuck some loose hair behind my ear. I nod back at him enthusiastically and he stands up, placing my feet back on the ground.

"Come on then, let's go get ya that burger that'll change your life." His concern morphs into a smile as he takes my hand and leads me out the door.

———————

I'm surprised by my own excitement as Mitch drives through the drive-thru and orders our food. I sit safe and secure in the passenger seat beside him, watching all the hustle and bustle going on around us. Families are piling into the restaurant together, there's a line of cars behind us ready to give their orders, and while Mitch waits for our food to be ready, he takes my hand in his and squeezes it tight.

"You're doin' real good," he assures me, looking proud. I love the sense of achievement it gives me, it makes pushing myself to do these things worth it.

I watch a little girl come out of the restaurant door holding her daddy's hand. She giggles when he scoops her up and lifts her up onto his shoulders, and it makes me smile for so many different reasons. I'll bet she has a whole bunch of fairytale books in her room, that her mother reads to her at night before she kisses her and tucks her under the covers. I'll bet the man who carries her on his shoulders feels like the luckiest man in the world, just like Mitch would have been with his own son if he'd had the chance to know him at that age. I'll also guarantee that the woman who follows them behind carrying a balloon cries sometimes for no other reason than the love she feels in her heart. I remember that feeling of overwhelming love and I never even got to meet my baby.

"Evy, you okay?" Mitch looks worried when I turn back to face him, and when I feel the tear slip over my cheek I quickly wipe it away with the heel of my palm.

"I'm fine." I put on a smile for him

"Darlin', you're cryin', if this is too much—"

"Happy tears," I interrupt him, shaking my head and watching as the family get inside the car on the other side of the parking lot. Seeing scenes like I just did help me know for sure that all the things we were told by the elders were untrue. There is good in the world outside. People smile, people are happy, and they take care of each other.

"Well, you're about to get a lot happier." He reaches out the car window when the lady on the other side passes him our order, and after dumping it on the console between us he pulls away.

"I got the perfect spot to take ya to enjoy this," he tells me.

We drive for about fifteen minutes until the buildings disappear and the roads become narrow again. Mitch takes a left down a long, narrow track and when we get to the bottom of it there's a huge cliff edge in front of us. I hold my breath as he spins the truck and parks with the tailgate facing out over the view.

"Come on." He reaches onto the back seat and grabs a rolled-up sleeping bag, then picking up our food he gets out the truck. I follow after him and look out at the view in front of us, it's all landscape that never seems to end. Mountains behind mountains that fade into the distance and when he pulls the tailgate down and taps the bed, I realize that he wants me to sit on it.

"Dinner and a view." He smiles as he lays out the sleeping bag, and when I step closer to him I let him lift me up and place me on the flatbed. He jumps up beside me and sets out our food for us, then laughs at the noises I make when I discover that Savannah tells no lies. This food is incredible. Maybe I should be ashamed of the fact I finish mine way before Mitch does, but I have no regrets. I've been deprived of these kinds of things for far too long. Why shouldn't I embrace them?

"We don't have to hurry back, do we?" I look back out at that view and notice that the sun is slowly starting to disappear behind the mountains. The orange and purple in the sky combine and make the vision in front of me look like something from a picture in a book.

"We got all the time in the world." Mitch wipes his mouth with a napkin and shoves our rubbish out of the way, before his arm curls around my shoulder and he tucks me into his body.

"I told everyone at the ranch today that you were my girl." He eventually breaks the silence, almost sounding guilty. I smile to myself because I really like the way it sounds. "I didn't feel bad for it," he confesses, causing me to look up at him and wonder what he means. "I'm done with all that, now." He stares down at me with eyes focused and sincere. "Look at ya, you came out tonight, you're sittin' on tailgate watchin' the sun go down, and you're smilin'. All I've wanted since I first saw ya, is for ya to be happy. For ya to see the beauty in this world and not to fear it, and if this is what makes you happy and is gonna keep that smile on your face, I'll leave all my insecurities behind me too. I'll do everything I can to give you the life you deserve." He takes my face in his hand and draws me closer and when our lips touch and that thrill starts to stir in my stomach, I decide to embrace the moment. I slide my leg over his and straddle his hips, deepening our kiss and making it a lot more intense. So intense that I feel him harden beneath me. It puts a rush in my blood that makes me more determined to explore my boundaries.

There's no one around us, the air is still warm and when I think about all the hurdles I still have left to jump, I decide to leap over the biggest one of them all. Pulling myself slightly away from him, I sit back on his lap then watch him look at me in confusion as I slowly lift my top up over my head and reveal all the marks Abraham put on my body.

His eyes soften as he studies them and I have to look away because I don't want to see him grimace at me. Up to now, every step we've taken has been so beautiful and enlightening. I guess we have to face up to some of the ugly if I want to keep moving forward.

"Hey." Mitch pinches my chin between his thumb and finger, forcing me to look back at him. "Don't look away from me like you're ashamed of this." His hand slides down my neck and arches around my throat, while the hand he had resting on my hips softly slides over my mutilated skin, tracing the burn marks and the scars Abraham put there. He pulls me back onto his lips, then wraps his arm around my body and brings me in tighter, letting his hands roam across my back covering more wounds that will never heal. He kisses my neck, grazing me with his teeth, while his hands continue to explore, and as his mouth lowers further down my body he gently pushes me back so he can get better access to me. Touching his mouth delicately over all my hideous marks as if he can make them vanish.

"Mitch. You don't have to..." I push against his shoulder. "I just wanted you to see what I am." I smile at him sadly and when he furrows his brow, I wonder what he's thinking.

"These scars ain't what you are, Evy, they're just a part of your story."

"I know they're ugly," I whisper, still trying not to cry.

"Not to me they ain't." His fingertip traces over the angry red line that came from Abraham's fishing hook. "There ain't an ugly thing about you." He lifts my hips up so he can kiss me there too, and the rush it gives me makes me even more determined to break down my barriers.

"I want you." I bite my lip nervously, not quite knowing what I'll do if he rejects me.

"I told ya, darlin', you got me." He chuckles to himself.

"Not just like this, I want us to be together, fully together." I look between us where he's hard and pressing between my legs. "I want to feel you inside me. I want to belong to you."

Mitch slowly nods his head and looks very serious.

"I'd like that too." He strokes his thumb over my cheek and smiles as if he's nervous too. "I guess we should get back home."

"No." I shake my head back at him. "Here, like this." I slide my fingers over the buckle of his belt, praying that he won't deny me. I'm calm and comfortable, surrounded by beautiful things that I never thought I'd have the chance to see. This moment feels right.

"Ev, when this happens it should be done properly. Not on a flatbed of a truck out in the open." Now he really looks nervous.

"This is perfect, it's just you and me." I look at all the space around us and take his hand, placing it over one of my breasts. Just the way he squeezes it makes my pussy throb like it's missing something.

"Mitch, I'm ready," I assure him with a smile.

"Ya sure?" He frowns. "Because I don't wanna get this wrong, the second you—"

"You won't get it wrong, you always know what I need." I go to slide off him and lie back but he holds me firm, preventing me from moving.

"You should be in control of this," he tells me, loosening his hold to unbuckle himself and open up his jeans. "You take what ya want, Evy, you control the pace, you decide when we stop." He nods at me.

Taking his cock in his hand he lets it spring out between us. And when his fist bunches up my skirt and pushes it up to my waist, I feel the head of his cock brush against my panties. "Just that feels nice," I laugh at myself. Starting to wonder if I will be able to take him all inside me.

"How about this?" Mitch hooks my panties to one side and allows his cock to slide inside them, his thick tip sliding between my folds and bringing a little relief to the ache inside me.

"It's nice." I nod back, starting to move my hips to get more of it.

"You're gettin' real wet." He reaches up his hand and slips his fingers into my mouth. "Wet these for me too," he orders, and when I suck hard at his fingers I feel his cock pulse against me.

"You're so damn perfect, don't ever let anyone tell ya anythin' different." He uses the fingers I just wet to stroke away the tension that I feel pulsing on the outside, his fingers and his cock working in the perfect sequence to build something up inside me that I've never experienced before.

"Mitch, what's happening?" My hips seem to be moving on their own now, as if my body knows what it needs but my head hasn't caught up.

"Mitch." I slam my hand into his shoulder and grip tight because I don't know what to expect.

"Fuck, Evy, I gotta taste it. Rest your hands against the back of the cab," he tells me as he quickly shimmies his body low enough for his head to rest between my legs. I'm glad that I did as he said when I feel his warm, wet tongue replace his cock and fingers. My whole body jolts when I feel one of his fingers slip inside me as his mouth kisses and his tongue strokes between my legs. Whatever it is that's been building inside me gets even stronger, turning into a wave of pleasure that I have no choice but to ride. My body tingles and my stomach feels on fire as I lose all control of myself. I cry out but not from pain, from something very different, and unlike anything I've ever encountered before. I never want it to end and I slam my hand against the back of Mitch's truck cab when it starts to sustain. Mitch slides himself back up to me wearing a huge grin on his face.

"I'm gonna take it that you enjoyed that."

I grab him and kiss him, unsure what it was, or how he managed it, but so grateful for it that I could cry. What Mitch just gave me is proof that no matter what's been done to me in my past, I can find pleasure in our connection.

"I'm ready," I whisper, feeling as if my chest is going to explode from all the excitement inside it. Any nerves I had are gone. All I want now is to be connected with Mitch.

"Okay, darlin'." Suddenly the smile drops from his lips and Mitch looks serious again. "But you stop whenever you need to. You're in control, remember?" he reminds me, taking his cock in his hand and guiding it toward my opening. His head nods at me once I feel him in place, pressing hard against me and threatening to stretch me with his size. I already know it's going to hurt, but it's a pain I want, one I've chosen to take and so I steadily lower myself over him.

"Grrrr, Jesus Christ, you're tight," Mitch growls, holding on to my hip as I slip more and more of myself over him. It stings a little, but the soft stroke of his hand against my thigh and the encouragement on his face, seem to make it all tolerable.

"I'm sorry, I have to take it slow." I bite my lip.

"Don't apologize. I like it. I wanna feel every inch of ya," he tells me with tension in his eyes.

I smile back at him with a newfound confidence, resting my palms on his strong chest and dropping my body enough to take him all the way. His hold on me becomes much more strained, and the veins in his arms bulge and he closes his eyes and holds his breath.

"Are you okay?" I check, wondering how could I have gotten this wrong.

"I'm fine." His voice comes out raspy. "It's just, you feel *so* fuckin' good." My stomach aches from where I hold him inside me, especially when I start to laugh in relief, and when Mitch joins me, he curls his hand around the back of my neck and pulls me down so our foreheads are touching.

"That's the most beautiful sound in the world, ya know that?" he whispers. "And this?" he rolls his hips and stirs himself inside me. "Fuckin' perfect."

I move slowly and steadily so that I adjust to his size, and eventually I gain more confidence. The bed of the truck starts to rock with us and Mitch keeps his eyes on mine, looking at me as if what we're sharing is different for him too. There's an overwhelming sense of strength in my chest that even manages to override the pleasure that's starting to build in my stomach again.

"Why ya cryin', darlin?" Mitch slides both his hands between our faces and brushes away my tears with his thumbs, cradling my head and making me feel like the most precious thing in the world.

"I'm just... happy." I laugh through my tears and keep my thrusts against him soft and steady. "This is what it feels like to love someone, isn't it?" I don't care that I'm giving too much of my feelings away to him, I want him to have everything I have to give. Because even in a world without masters, I want to belong to him.

"I think it is." He nods back at me confidently, then kisses me until that pleasure inside me unleashes and I scream loud enough to make the Heavens shake. Mitch's fingers dig into my flesh, and he growls deep as he holds himself still inside me.

The cold drops that start to splash against our skin don't seem to bother us, but after another rumble from the clouds, they come down heavier and much faster.

"Shit, we better get back inside." Mitch quickly rolls me off him and slides back down to the tailgate, tucking himself away before aiding me off the back. He follows me to the passenger seat, holding the sleeping bag over my head to protect me from the rain. I'm already wet but it's the thought that matters and when I'm safely in the cab, I wait for him to move around the truck and jump in the driver's seat. He tosses my shirt at me and seeing us both drenched through to our skin makes us both erupt with laughter.

"Come here." He leans across the console, hooking his finger under my chin and pulling me to him for a kiss.

"I wish every day could be like this one," I whisper once he pulls away and gets ready to drive. I notice the blue flash of lightning light up the sky, but it doesn't scare me the way it used to when it lit up the cracks in the door to the bunker.

"I'll do my best," Mitch promises, before starting the engine and driving us home.

CHAPTER 21

MITCH

Hunter is riding Everleigh's horse around the corral when I get to the ranch the next morning, and the others are making their usual attempts to look busy. I move past them all to find Garrett, and he's looking furious when I find him chopping wood over by the wood store.

"Whoa, who got on the wrong side of you?"

"Bianca fuckin' Mason, that's who." He throws the ax into the wood stump before he kicks it.

"Chill the fuck down and tell me what's goin' on." I stare at him in confusion.

"That bitch invited Maisie to her stupid garden luncheon party. She's playin' games." He shakes his head as he lights himself up a smoke.

"Well, it ain't like Maisie hasn't got a good excuse not to attend, she's got three little ones," I point out.

"She's also stubborn as fuck." Garrett trumps me. "She wants to go and *play her part*." He tosses his lighter across the ground when it's obvious that he's too agitated to spark it.

"Here, calm down." I take my lighter out and spark it for him, holding it up so he can light his smoke, and once he takes a deep inhale of nicotine I feel him calm down.

"Think about it, Garrett, what is Bianca gonna do to the mayor's wife in front of all the most important women in town? She had to invite her. It would have looked rude if she didn't. And that woman of yours has proven time and time again that she can hold her own. When is this party thing?"

"Sunday, after church." Garrett clenches his jaw so tight he can hardly get the words out. "And you better tell all them bunkhouse boys to pull out their Sunday bests, I want a presence in that chapel. And that includes you too."

"Garrett, you know I don't—"

"This Sunday, you do. I want *all* my boys lined up in those pews, showing what she'll have to face if she tries anythin'. Make it happen." He goes to walk away.

"Jesus Christ, Garrett." I slide my hand over my face, wondering how I'm gonna pull this off.

"That's the fuckin' spirit." He raises his hat to me before he heads back inside the ranch.

I spend the rest of the day doing my usual jobs, around the usual people, but everything seems so much different. I watch Hunter and how eager he is to get stuff done. Every now and then I'll catch him looking over at me and we smile at each other, not really knowing what to say. I think about Everleigh back at home, and how our lives are gonna change now. There's no more holding back for us. She's mine, now. I can kiss her when I want, hold her in my arms when I know she needs it. With me she seems to have no doubts and last night all barriers between us got destroyed. Nothing in this world is gonna stop me from keeping her happy.

The day doesn't drag as long as I thought it would and when it's time for me to saddle up and ride home, I'm about to jump on JD when a car skids into the yard and Savannah climbs out the driver's seat.

"Afternoon, Mitch." She slides her sunglasses up into her

hair and winks at me as she passes on her way into the main house.

"Afternoon." I raise my hat.

"Everleigh okay, today?"

"Oh, I think you know the answer to that." She sniggers as she makes her way straight to Cole and stretches up on her toes to kiss him. I shake my head at her as I leap up onto JD's back and ride the hell outta there.

Everleigh is humming in the kitchen when I step inside, the place is a mess, but it smells like homemade cookies.

"What happened here?" I take a look at the carnage around us.

"Savannah was telling me that there's a bake sale at the church on Sunday. I thought I'd send a contribution."

"Well, that's kind of ya." I move straight for her, picking her up and landing her on the kitchen surface. Then I kiss her like I've been wanting to all day.

"You and Savannah discuss anything else?" I raise my eyebrow at her.

"Of course. I told her that I absolutely agree that those burgers were to die for." She teases me with her nose and then giggles when I tickle her ribs. Anyone looking at her right now would never know that she was treated so terribly and I wish Jimmer could be here to see how far she's come.

"You don't mind that we talk, do you?" She creases her forehead like she's suddenly become concerned.

"Of course, I don't mind. I think it's nice you have a friend. Hopefully, that will extend to the other girls too." I kiss her some more because I can't get enough of her lips.

"I was also thinking, maybe you should invite Hunter here

for dinner. You can't really get to know him while you're working, and I'd like to meet him." She smiles up at me and I fall a little bit harder.

"I think that's a great idea." I suddenly realize that I've purposely been avoiding him today. It's not because I don't want him around. I just have no idea what to say, or how to make up for all that lost time. But Everleigh's right, he should come here and we should be getting to know each other better.

"Great, we'll have corn dogs and I'll make homemade burgers." She looks infectiously excited and when I lift her up off the work surface and carry her toward the bedroom, her eyes glisten with even more of it.

"I've missed you today." I lay her down on the mattress and hang my hat on the bedpost.

"I really missed you too." She looks up at me expectantly and when I drop to my knees and slip the dress that she's wearing up her thighs, I slide my tongue over the skin I expose.

"Mitch." She holds it down, preventing me from pushing it up past her waist.

"What?" I hold back, worrying that I've done something wrong.

"I took my top off last night because it felt unfair to hide it from you. You don't have to look at it every time." She shakes her head sadly, putting a wedge in my throat and digging a splinter into my heart.

"You don't get it, do ya?" I slide up from the floor so my body hovers over hers, then sliding her dress further up her body I reveal each scar and mark that fucker put on her. "I love every single part of you, these included. Sure, I hate how ya got 'em, but each one of these..." I trail them with my fingertips as she holds her breath. "Are evidence of how strong you are. You survived each day and now I'm gonna make sure it was worth it. These scars make me more and more in awe of ya, and I never want ya to be ashamed of them again." I finish sliding the dress all the way over her head, unclasping her bra and slipping it over her shoulder, then taking her tits in my hands I squeeze at them gently. She looks up at me and smiles as she reaches between us and slides her fingers into my waistband, rubbing her palm against my hard cock and making me even more desperate to be inside her.

I get straight to work unbuckling my belt and forcing my jeans off, then letting my heavy cock rest against her stomach so she can continue to slide her palm over my shaft.

"You do that so fuckin' well," I growl, hanging my head into her neck so I can look down and watch.

Her scars don't seem to matter to her anymore, she's too focused on our connection.

"You wanna feel me inside ya, darlin'?" I check, lifting both her legs over one of my shoulders so I can slide her panties up over her ankles.

She lies back on the mattress and nods at me, and I wonder if she knows that she's taken my whole world and turned it on its head. I wonder if she knows that every breath I take now seems to be for her. This beautiful, broken girl, with scars on the inside and out, has become the start and end of my world, along with everything in between. My purpose in the life I've been given is to make her forget every awful thing that happened before me.

"Okay, sweetheart." I twist my head to kiss her ankle, keeping my arm anchored around both her thighs as I slip my cock inside her. We both make the same relieved sound as I fill up her tight, little channel. Her legs are high on my shoulder, forced together, making it feel as if she's squeezing me inside her. She must feel so full, but the moans she's making are all outta pleasure. I love how it feels to be the one consuming her.

"You look adorable takin' my cock," I tell her, guiding her

hips and thrusting a little harder, "So fuckin' pretty, it hurts." I kiss the foot that's resting beside my ear as I glide my hand up her smooth, milky legs and clasp her ankles together tightly. "I'm so proud of how far you've come," I whisper, wishing she could know just how much.

I release her legs, allowing them to fall apart and take up the space between them with my body, remaining inside her and taking one of her rose-colored nipples to my mouth. I suck it hard and flick it with my tongue, loving the way her body responds. Tiny sparks of thrill flickers in her eyes as I roll my hips deeper and deeper into hers and when her nails dig into my back, I reach over my shoulder to pull the shirt off over my head so we're skin-to-skin. She looks between us, watching how my cock slips in and out of her.

The look on her face suggests she's proud of herself. I'll bet there was a time when she thought this would be impossible too. I don't know who the fuck I have to thank for bringing us together despite us being worlds apart, but there can be no more doubt and no more confusion. This is right, our pasts don't matter, our ages are insignificant. She's the piece of the puzzle that I never knew I was missing and it suddenly dawns on me that after all these years of protecting myself, I've fallen completely and mercifully in love, and there's no climbing back from it.

The past few days I've been floating on a cloud, me and Mitch have spent all our free time exploring each other's bodies, and the past has never felt so far away. I can sense an unease in him this morning though, and when I finish tidying up after breakfast I'm shocked and almost knocked off my feet when he comes out of the bedroom wearing a suit.

"Wow." I look him up and down and wonder how it's possible to be that handsome. It seems he can pull off any look he wants.

"Yeah, well, don't get used to it," he growls miserably as he uses the mirror to straighten his tie.

"Is going to church what's got you in such a bad mood?" I ask him, unable to resist moving over to him to be closer.

"I ain't in a bad mood." He frowns at me and when I raise my eyebrow at him he sighs. "Okay, I hate church." He shrugs, moving away from the mirror and over to his chair so he can polish his shoes. I perch on the end of the couch beside him and wait for him to tell me why.

"Don't get lookin' at me like that, I know your appreciation for the man upstairs, and just because I don't say my prayers or go to church every Sunday and sing my lungs out, don't mean I ain't got it either. I just don't. Like. Church." He puts all his aggression into his polishing.

"So why go?" I ask.

"Because thirty-two years ago I took a brand and a vow to be wherever a Carson needs me to be." He shakes his head.

"I'm sure Garrett would understand, is it a special occasion?" I'm not entirely sure how churches out here in the real world run, but Mitch is obviously feeling the pressure to be there today.

"No, just a plain old Sunday service. There's a woman who's come to town and is playin' some mind games."

"The one who sent the head?"

"The..." Mitch looks stunned by my knowledge. "How did ya... Savannah." He shakes his head and looks even angrier.

"Mitch, you don't have to keep things from me. I got a pretty good idea that this place wasn't your run-of-the-mill ranch when I saw that brand on your chest. You don't have to hide anything from me."

"Well, she's invited Garrett's wife to some fancy luncheon after church and Maisie is insistent on goin'." I can tell he's not impressed by that.

"Garrett wants us to have a strong presence in church today. Leia and Savannah are helpin' with the bake sale after, and he wants eyes everywhere. So, here I am, dressed up like a dog's dinner ready to sing my praises." He shakes his head furiously.

"So why do you hate church so much?" I know from what Savannah has told me that Mitch has endured way worse than an hour in church for the Carson cause.

"Church don't hold good memories for me, darlin'." He puts on his shoes and avoids eye contact.

"Do you wanna talk about it?" I ask, everyone I speak to

tells me that talking is the best way to get over my trauma, maybe it would work for Mitch too.

"No, I don't." He stands up and I quickly take his hand.

"Please, Mitch. I don't like us having secrets."

"You really wanna know?" He sighs, and when I nod he sits back down and squeezes my hand.

"When I was a boy my parents used to take me and my sister to church every Sunday. My mom and sister would dress immaculately, my father would polish his shoes, and mine, to ensure we all looked our best. We'd smile, we'd talk to everyone in the congregation. Then we'd come home. Dad would drink, and Mom would pay for it. Every Sunday was the same." He clears his throat as the bad memories come back alive inside his head.

"I'm sorry you had to go through that." I place my other hand over the one I have linked with his.

"Did they separate?" I'm curious about where they are now. Mitch never talks about his parents.

"No, when his beatin's started to extend to my sister, Mom started fightin' back. One argument got outta hand and Dad ended up pushin' Mom down the stairs. My sister was only young and I remember her screamin', beggin' her to wake up. The ambulance took her and she was in a coma for three weeks, just lyin' there asleep.

Dad visited every day, actin' like a lovin' husband, pretendin' it was an accident and willin' her to come back to us. But I knew she was gone."

"Mitch." I can't imagine how awful it must have been to watch someone you love die like that.

"He told me to stick to the story that she fell, and said if I didn't, child services would take Harriet away and I'd never see her again."

"And did you?"

"I stuck to his story, I hugged my sister when they turned Mom's life support off then I held her hand while she got buried into the ground."

"And do you speak to your father now?" I ask, fascinated by the past Mitch has had. I knew he had a nephew, but he never mentioned a sister before.

"My father's dead," he rasps, sliding his hand through his beard.

"And did you make peace with him before he died?" I know from reading the Bible that forgiveness is strength, it sets you free. It's what I keep searching for whenever I think of my sister.

"Everleigh..." Mitch grips hold of me as if he's scared I'll run away. "I'm the one who killed him." His expression is blank as he waits for my reaction.

S he says nothing in response, just stares back at me, and I instantly regret being so damn honest when she stands up and heads toward the bedroom. Slouching back in my chair I scrub my hand over my face in frustration. What was going through my head when I admitted that? Things are good between us. So fuckin' good, and now I've ruined it. I've never tried to hide who I am from Everleigh, but there are some things that you just have to hold back.

I hear the door click a few minutes later and when I see that Everleigh has changed into a cute, floaty dress that almost touches the floor, I study her up and down as she stands herself in front of me.

"Come on." She holds out her hand, and despite my utter confusion, I take it.

"Come where?"

"To church, I'm coming with you." She has a strong, determined look on her face, and it makes the hairs on the back of my neck stand up.

"Evy, most of the town shows up for church, it's full of people, and—"

"I want to be there for you, just like you're always there for me. And I don't care about the people, not when I've got you to hold my hand."

"You're serious, ain't ya?" I shake my head, wondering where the hell this woman gets her strength from.

"Of course, I'm serious. I told you, I want to prove that I can do this."

"You don't have to prove anythin' to me," I tell her, standing up and taking both her elbows in my hands.

"Well, maybe I need to prove it to myself. I want to do this for both of us." I feel the smile pick up on my face before I kiss her, then allowing her to take a deep, brave breath I keep my hand in hers and lead her out the door.

"You just say when it gets too much. Okay?" Mitch smiles as he gets out of the driver's seat and rounds the hood so he can open my door. "You're in control," he reminds me, taking my hand and leading me toward the group of people who are gathered on the lawn in front of the chapel.

"Everleigh?" Savannah looks as shocked as she is excited to see me and nearly takes me out with the huge hug she greets me with.

"Maisie, Leia, this is Everleigh." She still seems stunned as she introduces me and both women greet me with warm smiles and kind eyes. "I had no idea you were coming today." She beams at me.

"It was a last-minute decision." I try to stay engaged and ignore the crowd of people around me. But I still feel everyone's eyes judging me.

"Well, we're glad you did, we've been wanting to meet you," Leia tells me, and as if Mitch can sense my discomfort he wraps his arm around my waist and pulls me in close.

"That there is baby Dalton, he's named after my nephew and his uncle." He gestures his head into the stroller that Leia is holding onto. "And Garrett over there is holding little Brianna. Where are the boys?" he asks Maisie, looking around for them.

"Cole took them for a walk to get them off to sleep," Maisie informs him, then leans closer to me and lowers her voice. "They aren't big fans of church."

"We were just telling Maisie to stop panicking about her dress, she's nervous about Bianca's stupid party," Savannah pipes up.

"Will you keep your voice down?" Maisie whisper-yells at her friend. "It's just been a while since I wore anything fancy, and this isn't exactly comfortable." She tugs on the bottom of the tight-fitted dress she's wearing. "I think it's far too short for church."

"It's the perfect length, and I'm sure God doesn't mind a little thigh. Why else would he have given ya such nice ones?" Savannah points out, making both me and Leia smirk at each other. Mitch slots his hand into mine and squeezes gently when everyone starts moving through the chapel doors, and Savannah gives me another quick hug.

"I'm so freaking proud of you," she whispers, before waddling over to join the guy who's pushing the double stroller from the other side of the lawn.

"You good?" Mitch checks as he leads me inside and I nod back at him because I actually am. Yes, having all these people surrounding us feels a little overwhelming, but I can tell just from meeting the girls that they are kind like Savannah, and having Mitch by my side makes me feel capable of getting through anything.

———

The service is much different from the ones we had at the village. Abraham would rant at his congregation and victimize people for their sins, sometimes there would be lashings if he wanted to make an example out of someone. Here in Fork River, I find myself intrigued by the words the preacher speaks. In fact, I find all he has to say very insightful. Maisie still looks nervous when the service is over, and when Leia and Savannah take all three of her little ones so she can leave for her party I notice they're going to have their hands full, especially considering they are helping with the bake sale.

"Can I help?" The words stumble out of my mouth, shocking everyone around me.

"Sure." Leia smiles as she finishes wrestling one of Maisie's boys back into his stroller. "There's always room for an extra set of hands."

"Garrett is dropping me off at the Mason ranch now, make sure you call if you need me." Maisie kisses her babies goodbye.

"You don't have to do this," Garrett speaks under his breath as he stands in front of her.

"That bitch sent a rotting head to my house. I'm doing this." She fixes a fake smile on her lips as she looks across to the circle of smartly dressed women opposite us.

"Good to see ya." Garrett raises his hat at me, before taking his wife's arm and leading her over to his truck.

"I wish we could have gone with her." Savannah watches them leave, shaking her head.

"You're in no condition to be starting anything, besides, we want peace. This family has been through enough turbulence to last a lifetime," Leia points out.

"I second that." The man I assume is Savannah's husband comes from behind her and slides his hands around her rounded stomach. "I think ya should take the kids home and put your feet up, they got enough help for the bake sale." He kisses her cheek.

"Put my feet up? With these hell raisers? Cole, you have to be kidding." She looks at me and rolls her eyes.

"I just don't want you overdoin' shit."

"Thanks to Everleigh, I won't be, she's gonna help out too." Savannah reaches out and takes my hand. "Come on, these men can watch the kids and we'll see where we are needed. If not, we can just eat cake." I let her drag me away, looking over my shoulder to Mitch and smiling so he knows I'm okay.

There are lots of tables lined up around the town square and people are chatting while they tuck into all the homemade treats that are on offer. Leia is also child-free as she steps behind one of the tables and helps with the selling, and when I look back over to Mitch and his friends I see that Mitch has his eyes on me.

"You must be Everleigh." I have to strain my neck to look up at the man who stands in front of me. "I'm Hunter, I'm new too." He checks around him and looks awkward.

"Pleased to meet you." I hold out my hand the way everyone around here seems to when they greet each other.

"He said you invited me to supper and I just wanted to say thank you. The ranch has been busy and I've rarely had a chance to sleep let alone anything else, but I was hoping I could join ya tomorrow night."

"We'd like that." I smile up at him.

"Not like Mitch to have favorites," Savannah interrupts while scoffing on a brownie. "These are so good. They must be the ones I made." She winks.

"We'll see you tomorrow." I smile at Mitch's son before taking Savannah's arm and pulling her toward Leia, who looks like she could use some help.

I finish stacking the folded tables in the storage room behind the chapel and when I turn around and see her watching me, I stop what I'm doing and take her in.

"Do ya have any idea how proud I am of you today?" Moving toward her I slide my hand under her jaw and angle her mouth so I can kiss it. "Everleigh, ya never fail to surprise me," I tell her.

I stood back today and watched her in awe. It was her first time out in public and she took it in her stride. She even ended up helping to sell, and speaking to the folk of this town as if she's been here forever. Everleigh doesn't know it because she's been kept hidden for so long, but she's a people person.

"Cole and Wade have taken the kids home with Leia and Savannah," I explain, playing with the frill on the neckline of the pretty dress she's got on. It's unholy of me, but all I've thought about today is lifting it up and having her legs around my waist.

"Pretty much everyone's gone home. I wonder how Maisie's doing?" she asks.

"Garrett's scheduled to pick her up in an hour, he's been like a bear with a sore head."

"Leia told me he's got two of your bunkhouse boys watching the property," she tells me, and I'll bet she is wondering just how dangerous this woman is.

"I can believe it... and now, I understand it too." I hold her just that little bit tighter.

"What do you mean by that?" She looks back at me confused.

"What I mean is, that if I thought for one second that you were in any danger, I'd do whatever it took to protect you." I've always understood the Carson men's need to protect their women. I've aided them in it whenever I could, but now that I got something of my own to treasure I get how limitless it is. I'd burn this world down before I let it hurt her again.

"You know the whole town were talking today?" She slides her dainty, little hand over my tie. "Apparently it's not every day Mitch Hudson turns up somewhere with a woman on his arm." She's wearing a mischievous smile.

"It ain't, now ya know how lucky you are." I glide my thumb across her cheek and wonder how an old man like me has become so utterly obsessed.

"I feel lucky." The look she gives me back is serious and so fuckin' grateful that it scrapes another groove into my heart.

"*I'm* the one that got lucky." I check there's no one around before dragging her into the storage room and pressing her back against the wall. I kiss her deep and hard, just like I've been craving all day, and after losing my belt and opening the front of my slacks I lift her up and hook her legs around my waist.

"You wanna do that here?" She looks as shocked as she is thrilled.

"Right here," I assure her, using the weight of my body to keep her top half pinned to the wall, so my hands can explore her.

Sex with Everleigh has become my new addiction and I'm starting to believe it's becoming hers too.

"Mitch, isn't this part of the chapel?" she whispers, her cheeks flushing pink.

"I'm aware of that." I hook my fingers into her panties and drag them to one side, letting the tip of my cock press against her. "We could wait until we get home if you want?" I tease her by pressing inside her, just a fraction.

"I think God will understand." She kisses me frantically, and as I push myself all the way inside her I feel the cold rush of relief slip over my skin.

Everleigh looks like a fuckin' vixen keeping her eyes connected with mine, luring me in and tempting me more. This woman shocks me every day with what she's capable of and today has just proven that her past won't destroy her.

"Don't be gentle with me," she warns. "I want it rough. I trust you." I don't wanna push her limits, but at the same time I don't wanna deny her, so I take her throat in the arch of my hand and apply just enough pressure to pin her to the wall. My thrusts become harder, so hard that the shelves start to shake, and when Everleigh starts to moan a little too loud I reach up over her chin and shove three of my fingers into her mouth.

"Suck 'em," I order, fuckin' her mouth as well as her pussy and feeling her soak me. I wait until my fingers are drenched before sliding them between us and using them to massage her clit. Her eyes widen as her pussy clamps tight around me and just seeing the pleasure on her face has me coming along with her. I hold her tight to me as we both come down and when we hear footsteps approaching, followed by Dolores's voice, I quickly pull outta her and tuck my cock back in my slacks.

"What's taking so long? We still have five tables to put away." She pops her head around the corner and despite making herself decent, Everleigh still looks horrified.

"I was just stackin' 'em up right so we can get 'em all in," I inform her, taking Everleigh's hand and leading her back out.

"And you needed help with that, did ya?" She looks Everleigh up and down with a knowing smile on her face.

"Of course, I did. Every man needs a strong woman beside him." I wink at the old woman and lead my girl back outside.

I've played nice all afternoon, engaged in small talk with the rest of Bianca's specially selected guests, and listened to her brag about all the things she's achieved in her life. I even took time to admire the modern art that she's revamped the Mason ranch with, all while wishing I was back at the bake sale with people I actually like.

Time passes fast now, and it's only five minutes until Garrett will be here to pick me up. So when Bianca excuses herself from her guests and heads for the kitchen for more champagne, I take my opportunity and follow after her.

"Leave us." I look to the girl who's been waiting on us and gesture my head toward the door, then focusing all my attention on Bianca I step closer.

Her eyes double in size when I wrap my hand under her jaw and dig my nails into her flesh.

"My husband was far too polite when he came here the other day. Now, I'll tell you what he should have said." I stare the nasty bitch straight in her eyes and clench my fingers tighter. "If you *ever* make a threat to my family again, your head will be the next one that's rolling loose. My husband may be too much of a gentleman to hurt a woman, but I'm happy to take a bitch down. You'd think the Masons would learn from past experiences that you can't win a war with the Carsons." I hold her face a little longer and smile at her. "Stay away from my family." I release her, lifting the bottle of champagne off the work surface and knocking some back before I push open the door and head back into the living room.

"I'm ever so sorry, I have to cut the afternoon short. I must get back to my little ones." I smile at all the other women politely, before heading for the door and leaving.

Garrett is waiting for me on the drive with his shoulders propped against his truck and his arms folded. I smile at him as he opens the passenger door for me.

"How was it?" He offers me his hand before I step up.

"Fun." I shrug as I settle into my seat.

"Fun?" He looks unconvinced as he rounds the hood and starts his engine. "Yeah, real good fun." I feel much lighter as he pulls away and heads for home.

It's not just the Carson men who are prepared to do whatever it takes...

"So have you had any luck tracking down your mother?" I address the elephant in the room once we've all finished up with dinner. We've covered just about every subject that isn't related to the fact Mitch and Hunter are father and son, and it's not something that should be ignored. I think it's incredible that they've found each other, and tonight's proven that they share the same kind of interests. Mitch has done nothing but talk about how great Hunter is to have on the ranch, so I know how proud of him he is.

"Unfortunately, not." Hunter looks deflated as Mitch lifts up his plate and takes it to the sink. "Da— I mean Mitch had one of his friends look into her but they couldn't find anything dated after my adoption. It's as if she just vanished." Hunter lowers his eyes as Mitch retakes the table.

"We'll find her." He grips the boy's shoulder and gives him some assurance. "In the meantime, you keep up your hard work. I ain't ever seen someone pick up as quick as you do. You're gonna be handy when we do the cattle drive next month." Mitch changes the subject back to work again, and as happy as he looks to receive the praise, I also get the sense that Hunter was hoping for more from tonight. He didn't come here to be a bunkhouse boy. He came here to spend time with his father.

Hunter stays another hour, drinks a few scotches, and listens to some of Mitch's stories, most of which include the Carson brothers or his nephew Dalton. They laugh together, but behind all the smiles I see that they both regret that they've missed out on making their own memories. It's neither of their fault and something that they will both have to make up for, now that they've found each other.

It's later than usual when me and Mitch go to bed, and once we're snuggled under the covers I decide to get something off my chest.

"You can talk about her, you know."

"Talk about who?" Mitch settles his arm around me and places kisses in the dip between my neck and shoulder.

"Hunter's mother." I turn to face him so he can't shy away from it. "I understand that you had a life before me, that you've had women, it wouldn't upset me if you had some answers for him. I know you are doing everything you can to find her, but you can share what you do know about her, don't hold back because you're scared of hurting my feelings."

"Everleigh." He smiles at me sadly and strokes his hand through my hair. "I'm sad to say I don't know anythin' about her, other than the fact she lived in this town and lied to me about her age. Before you, I never paid much attention to females, not even the ones I brought home. I don't know how many nights we shared, or where it happened. I was young back then and always lookin' for a quick thrill. I wish I had answers for the boy, but I don't." I can tell he's disappointed in himself so I quickly change the subject.

"He worships you, you know?" I smile fondly when I think about the way he looked at Mitch. It's obvious that the boy aspires to be him. "We should have him over more often, and you shouldn't keep it a secret."

"We ain't keepin' it a secret, we're just waitin' for the test results to be sure, then I'll tell the whole yard, just like I did about you."

"How long for the results?" I ask through a yawn, it's been a long few days. Church really took it out of me yesterday and today I was brave enough to go with Savannah to the ranch to see Maisie and Leia again. It was fun, but like Mitch warned, very hectic.

"Any day now. I'm surprised they haven't come already. I must get on to the company." He tucks my head into his chest and rests his chin on top of my head. "Now, get some sleep. You must be tired." I don't answer him, just close my eyes and take in the comfort in having him with me.

Five Weeks Later

I'm riding the pastures on my way to work, whistling to myself, and feeling on top of the damn world. I left Everleigh on the doorstep waving me off and looking hot-as-hell in one of my shirts. I know Savannah is on her way over and no doubt the two of them will be discussing what happened out on the porch last night. Who needs a book now?

I change my direction when something in the distance catches my eye. Trotting over toward the old RV that's parked up near one of the storage buildings that are on Grid 7, I frown curiously when I see a woman hanging out washing on a makeshift line, and a guy talking intensely on a cell phone.

"You folks lost?" I call out as I approach them.

The woman smiles at me nervously, before picking a baby up from the floor while the man I'm assuming is her husband does me the courtesy of ending his call.

"Could say that, we ran into a spot of bother last night."

"Well, this is private land, Carson land ain't for tourists," I remind them, wondering how they got so far from the road.

"Apologies. We didn't mean to trespass. Engine started sounding hinkey as we were driving toward town, I was just

trying to find somewhere safe to spend the night for my family."
He turns to his wife and strokes the baby's head affectionately.

"Can't blame a man for that, there's a garage in town. I
know the owner's son, well. I'm sure I could have him come out
here and take a look so you can be on your way." This guy must
have caught me in a good mood because I'm being helpful.
"And I'm sure, if I speak to the boss he'll understand the
circumstances, he's got young un's of his own. Though there's a
guest house in town if you'd be more comfortable there."

"We got everything we need right here," He places his arm
around his wife and the picture-perfectness of it all makes me
feel real sad that Everleigh will never have that with me. I know
how much she'd like a family.

"Okay, then. Welcome to Copper Ridge, keep your wits
about ya, it's bear season." I drop my head to them, before
moving on and heading toward the ranch.

CHAPTER 29

EVERLEIGH

The diner isn't busy, but I seem to hear every noise around me while I wait for Mitch to come back from the bathroom. I feel my heartbeat regulate when he returns and passes me a menu.

"The food here's great, Dolores makes a good meatloaf." He leans forward on the table, while I study the menu trying to choose something from the long list of options. If I'd told the girl down in the bunker who lived on stale bread that one day she'd be spoilt for choice on what she ate, she would have laughed at me.

Hunter comes rushing in through the doors looking full of energy and when he slides into the booth beside Mitch, he slams a pile of posters on the table in front of him.

"I just sweet-talked the library chick into printing me off a bunch of these." He sits back looking pleased with himself. "Dolores, can I get a—"

"Black coffee with a shot of hazelnut," she finishes for him before getting to work.

"And what, exactly, is this?" I pick one of his leaflets up and study it.

"That is a picture of my mom when she lived here. I just

cut Mitch out. I'm figuring, in a town as small as this one, someone must have known where she went when her family left. She must have confided in a friend." He sounds hopeful, and as I study the picture harder I realize that I'm looking at someone I know.

"This girl, how old would she be now?" I check, shaking my head and feeling my pulse start to throb in my temples.

"Her sister said she was seventeen the last time she saw her. I'm twenty-five so... early forties." Hunter shrugs as he makes a guess.

"Oh, my god." I feel myself go light-headed.

"Evy, what's wrong?" Mitch looks worried and I have to swallow down the sick feeling that's rising to my throat.

"I know this girl... Woman." I shake my head.

"You know Naomi?" Mitch stares at me as if I've gone mad.

"That's not her name. The people in the village called her Kayla, and she was married to an elder."

"Hold on." Mitch takes both my trembling hands in his. "Are you tellin' me, that the woman in this picture was in your village?"

"Yes." I suddenly feel as if the diner walls are closing in on me. I thought I was free of that place, but it turns out it keeps on finding me.

"My mom was part of the cult?" Hunter shakes his head in disbelief.

"She was married to Eric. He was a well-respected elder. I remember her because she was kind. Though my mother never liked her much. Come to think about it, not many women in the village did, I always figured it was because they were jealous. She's maintained her looks despite aging. This is undoubtedly her."

"Jesus." Mitch massages the bridge of his nose like he's

developed a headache. While I let it sink in that there's been a connection between me and him all this time.

"We need to find her. Didn't you say the Souls never hurt women?" Hunter looks to Mitch for reassurance.

"Never," he confirms.

"Then all the women from that village must still be alive. We have to find some." Hunter sounds full of hope and as happy as I am for him, I can't allow myself to get dragged back there. I'm nowhere near recovered enough for that, and suddenly I feel the pressure of being the only one who can help him.

"Hunter, give us five." Mitch nods his head toward the door when he sees that I'm starting to panic, and when Hunter follows his order he reaches over the table and grabs both my hands.

"Evy, breathe. It's okay," he tells me confidently, though I can see from the look in his eyes that he's just as thrown by this as I am.

"How is this okay? Hunter's mother was from the village. I can't go back there." I shake my head frantically.

"No one would ever expect that. We have resources. I'll speak to Maddy again. Nothin' has to change." His strong hands stop mine from trembling and I allow myself to breathe long calming breaths.

"It's all gonna be okay, you're *never* revisitin' that place," he assures me again.

CHAPTER 30

NAOMI

"**W**ill *you shut that child up?*" Solomon shouts back at Annie who's doing her best to keep her son pacified. He's been sick for days now and Solomon refuses to let her take him to a doctor. No wonder the poor thing cries continuously.

"It's him, I'm telling you it's him." I stare out the windshield at the tall, handsome boy on the other side of the street. I take out the picture I have of him with the couple who raised him, at his graduation, and hold it up as a comparison. I'm ashamed to say I stole it from their house a few weeks ago when Solomon broke in looking for evidence of where my son was, and although I was punished by him for taking it, it was worth it. I can now be certain that the person I'm looking at is my son.

"I could go and talk to him?" I suggest.

"Talk to him?" Solomon laughs at me cruelly. "Kayla, these things take time, you can't just stroll on up to him and announce yourself as the woman who abandoned him. This just proves how unready you are for this world." He shakes his head in disappointment.

I've lived twenty-five long years wondering what my son would look like. I never got to hold him, he was snatched away from me the second he was born. I've never been permitted to speak about him, I was told I had to deny his existence. So, looking at him now and seeing how strong and handsome he's become makes me want to cry with joy.

"I don't understand why he's so important to you, now. I was told to forget about him."

"You were told that by your last leader, and look at the disaster his selfishness caused. Our entire village was destroyed. Elders are dead. You were lucky I was prepared to take you on as wives or you'd be left to find your own paths," Solomon reminds us, *again*.

"I just want to know why he's so important now. What if he doesn't want to come with us?"

"Kayla, where we are going, we need strength in numbers, me showing up at our new settlement with two useless women and a child makes me a burden. Your son is good stock, tall, and broad. Men will want to marry their daughters to him. The elders are much more likely to accept us if we have him." Solomon takes my hand.

"When you spoke to my sister, what did she say? She must have told you what brought him here. He looks so happy."

"Your sister barely said a thing. She was cagey and disrespectful," he reminds me of the punishment I got for that too.

"He will be happy at our new home. It's what has been pathed out for us." Solomon softens his voice to assure me, though I don't believe him. Since the attack on our village, he's been unhinged. He's convinced that after the death of his father, he is the new messiah. What he forgets is that he has no one to lead. My husband was taken by the men who rode bikes and wore leather. I can only assume, and hope, that he is dead after the years he made me suffer.

Myself and Eric never had children, he was aware that I

had birthed a child before I came to the village and he blamed my sins for us not being blessed. He also blamed me for the fact his other wives weren't blessed either, which started the rumor that I was cursed. The women in my village wouldn't talk to me or even look at me in case I spread the curse to them. I spent years being a stranger to everyone, living in the shadows and wondering what became of the beautiful, baby boy who I carried inside me for nine, precious months.

Now that I'm looking at him, I want to reach out and grab him. Tell him how loved he was before I even met him and that not a day has gone by when I didn't think about him.

Baby Samuel continues to cry and Solomon turns his aggression on to Annie.

"I told you to keep that child silent," he scolds her.

"I can't, I'm sorry. He's sick and he's hungry. If you just let me see a doctor—"

"We can't trust doctors, Annie. They would take the child and place him with another mother, just like they did to Kayla's boy, is that what you want?" he snaps, and when Annie shakes her head she looks to me helplessly. I wish I could tell her that I know that's not true, It wasn't the doctors that took my son from me. It was Solomon's dad and his elders.

Solomon composes himself and focuses his attention back to the diner across the street, and suddenly I see him shift in the driver's seat, shooting forward so his nose is almost pressed against the windshield.

"No," he whispers, looking stunned. "It can't be."

"What?" I look across the street trying to see what has him so mesmerized.

"God is great." He smiles as he shakes his head and laughs. "God is great!" He slams his fist on the console making me jump, and when I see Mitch Hudson and the small-framed woman whose hand he holds as he joins my son, I have to do a double take.

"Is that Elder Thomas's daughter?" I check I'm seeing right because all this has to be an illusion. "She died years ago. Killed herself after her sister escaped."

"That's what Abraham wanted people to believe," Annie informs me from the back.

"She was mine." Solomon watches in fascination as the man I knew, when life was fun and simple, opens his truck door for her. She kisses him before she jumps into the seat and I see the rage in Solomon stiffen his whole body. "You see that? Us coming here and looking for him has led us to her. The Lord planned this, He led me here, now all will be as it should." He settles back in the driver's seat with a dark smile on his face and that rage still dilating his pupils

"I got a surprise for you." I gently shake Everleigh awake. When her eyes blink open and she smiles at me, I kiss her.

"Isn't it a little early in the day for surprises?" She yawns.

"Never too early, Come on." I rip the covers off her and lift her robe off the chair beside the bed.

"You really are in a hurry." She giggles as I drag her through the house and when I open the door and she sees the horse I bought her, tethered to the porch, she stands and stares at it.

"Well, say somethin'." Hunter stands up from where he's been waiting on the bench. He's put just as much work into this mare as I have over the past few weeks, it's only right that he should be here to see her surprise.

"She's yours," I explain to Everleigh, taking her hand and moving her closer. "She's rideable, and I think the two of you are gonna get on real well."

"She's mine?" Everleigh looks at me as if she doesn't quite believe it.

"I noticed the two of you had a bond when I first brought her here. She made your eyes do that pretty, sparkly thing they do whenever you're fascinated by somethin', and well, I'd do just about anythin' to keep that sparkle in your eyes." I move in close enough to kiss her.

"Yuck." Hunter kills the moment. "You're showing your age with those lines, old man." He shakes his head at me.

"Oh yeah, and just how many females have you got atcha heels? Because I don't see none," I ask sarcastically.

"That's because I'm focused on work right now. We have the cattle drive tomorrow and I want to be ready for it."

I gotta admit I'm impressed with his answer, though I can tell something's been troubling him recently. Hunter's been spending much more time around here, and I've enjoyed being able to get to know him. Everleigh seems to feel comfortable around him too, which makes everything a damn sight easier. Though in the past few days, I've noticed Hunter withdrawing a little, it's something I intend to talk to him about later.

"Can I ride her now?" Everleigh asks, practically hopping with excitement.

"You're gonna need a few lessons, first, but soon," I promise.

"No one's ever gotten me anything like this before." Her eyes fill up with tears before she launches herself at me and flings her arms around my neck. "She's beautiful." She moves across to her so she can stroke her and just like I predicted, the mare takes her affection willingly.

"She needs a name. I've left that up to you," I tell her.

"A name..." Everleigh thinks to herself. "I think we'll call you Aurora." She speaks to her horse, then looking over her shoulder at me she smiles. It means 'new beginning'. I was helping Savannah pick names from the book yesterday," she explains, turning her focus back to the horse. The smile on her face makes all the early mornings and hard work seem worth it, and when I look across at Hunter and he's smiling too, I nod my appreciation to him.

Everleigh insists that Hunter stay for breakfast and when it's time for us both to leave and get some work done, I decide to talk to Hunter on the way to the ranch.

"You okay, son?" I ask once the cabin is in the distance.

"Yeah, fine." He tries far too hard to sound it.

"I was just wonderin' if maybe you're nervous about tomorrow with the cattle drive?"

"A little, maybe, but I'm excited too." He shrugs.

"And you still got no word on those results? They say you shoulda had 'em back a few weeks ago?" Hunter pulls his horse to a standstill and keeps his head low, proving that I ain't crazy. There is something wrong.

"I got 'em through last week." He breathes through his nose.

"Ahhhh." I get a sinking feeling in my stomach that I wasn't expecting when I realize what it is that's been troubling him.

"I was so sure, it was there in black and white, and then we met and—"

"I know, son." I try hard to keep my own disappointment at bay. I was really starting to get used to the idea of being this kid's dad.

"I didn't know how to tell ya, and I was scared that things would change. You've made me feel so welcome here and I—"

"Hey, nothin's gonna change." I slap him on his back. "You're a hard worker and a good kid."

"But I ain't *your* kid. Being him felt real special, like I had something to live up to. Now I don't have a clue who I am."

"Listen to me, just because we don't share the same blood don't mean that you don't belong here." I'm shocked at how disappointed I am, and having to show face right now ain't fuckin' easy.

"I just don't understand why she would have lied on that certificate. Why put your name?" He shakes his head, looking defeated.

"I don't know, kid." The mystery of it all gets to me too, but not nearly as much as knowing this boy ain't mine. "We'll figure it out, we'll find her and get to the bottom of it," I promise him.

"You're still gonna help me?" He looks up at me surprised.

"Hell yeah, I'm gonna help ya. Hunter, around here we take care of our own, and you're one of us now. Like it or not."

"Does that mean I get the brand?" His lips raise into a clever smirk.

"No, it does not mean you get the brand." I shake my head at him.

"So, what do I have to do?" Now I realize he's being serious I got a nasty taste in my mouth.

"You gotta make sacrifices and earn it, and you sure can't be screamin' like a pussy over severed heads." I play it down because this boy may not be my son, but I still care a whole lot about him. Dalton wanted to wear the brand his whole life, and getting it, ended him up dead. I won't make that same mistake twice.

"Come on, we don't wanna be late." I kick JD into a trot so the subject can close.

"How was your day?" I kiss Everleigh when I walk back through the door.

"It was good, me and Savannah went to Leia's cabin and we just hung out." She has a huge beam on her face as she plates up our dinner. "Her little boy is so cute, all the kids are. I can't believe I was here for so long before meeting them." She sits down at the table and clasps her hands to say her prayers. I watch her, wondering if there's a cruel bone in her body.

Me, on the other hand, I've spent my entire day feeling resentful. Resentful of Bill fuckin' Carson for having four boys and not appreciating them. That man never spent any time doing what a father should do, it was me and their grandfather, Hank, who taught 'em all they know. Back when I thought Hunter was mine I felt the weight of that guilt. I hated all the years we'd missed out on and I had a whole lotta plans for making up that time. I was gonna be a good father, or at least I was gonna try my damn best.

"You okay?" Everleigh looks at me concerned.

"Hunter ain't mine." I rip the Band-Aid straight off and when I see the shock on her face, I have to look away.

"How? The two of you are so... Are you sure?" She shakes her head in disbelief.

"He got the results last week and didn't wanna tell me." I smile sadly, placing down my fork because suddenly, I ain't hungry.

"And you're disappointed?" She reads my fuckin' mind.

"Yeah, I'm disappointed. I ain't ever thought about being a father before, hell, the idea petrified me. My life has always been this ranch, but I looked at that kid and felt real proud to call him mine." I can feel the tears welling up in my eyes so I shake my head and get back to eating.

"And did you tell him that?" Everleigh reaches across the table and holds my hand. "I'll bet Hunter is every bit as disappointed as you are." She smiles.

"He was, and I told him I'll still help him find his mom. I just don't understand why that girl would lie, and why the hell she'd pick me to put on that certificate. I can't make sense of it."

"You knew this girl, right?" Everleigh abandons her food and walks around the table to rest herself on my knee.

"I think she was young and scared and she knew that you were a good person, maybe that's what she wanted for her little boy," she tells me softly as she snuggles her body into mine and makes everything feel right with the world again. "Hunter may not be your son, but you haven't lost the chance to be someone special to him," she reminds me.

"I think I'd have been a good father," I admit, wrapping my arms around her waist to keep her close.

"You would have been a great father, and you're gonna be an incredible person for him to look up to." She sounds so dreamy and enthusiastic that I almost believe her.

"I don't know about that." I shake my head and laugh.

"I do. You're an incredible man, you only have to see the way those Carson brothers look at you. You need to remember I talk to the girls, now. You are loved by so many people, and whether Hunter is blood or not, he's become one of them."

I grab my girl's face and kiss her. Her attempts to find the good in every situation are endearing and damn adorable.

"And do ya know how loved you are?" I stand up, taking her with me as I head toward the bedroom because suddenly, I got a real urge to show her.

"And you're sure you're going to be okay?" Mitch checks, his eyebrows creasing up with worry.

"I'll be fine, I'm probably just a little nervous for you." I smile up at him and nod my head. We're in the middle of the yard and all the couples are saying goodbye to each other, the last thing I want is for Mitch to make a fuss.

"You don't have to be nervous for me, darlin', this is the shit I live for." He kisses me in front of everyone, leaving me blushing when he pulls away.

"We'll be back by nightfall." He winks. "You take care of my girl." He points his finger at Savannah as he jumps up on his horse.

"I gotcha." She comes over and wraps her hand around my shoulder.

"What's he so worried about?" She speaks under her breath.

"Nothing, I'm fine. I just got a little dizzy this morning when I got out of bed. You know how he can be." I stand with the girls and wave the men off, and there's a real buzz of excitement in the air. The men clearly love doing what they do, and I'm told after a cattle drive the Carson ranch party hard.

As soon as the men are out the gates, Maisie turns to us all, "Let the fun begin." She wiggles her eyebrows as she leads us all inside. I'm told by Savannah that the girls have made it their tradition to spend cattle run days together. They make enough food to feed an army when the cowboys return, and the drinks flow freely. I've never really drank alcohol before but I'm prepared to give it a try, like I am most things these days.

Leia's little sister minds the little ones in the living room while me, Leia, Savannah, and Maisie take to the kitchen and get started on the feast for later.

"It may seem like a lot, but you'd be surprised how much those cowboys can eat after a run. I need to find the big pot." Maisie scrambles through the cupboard in search of it, and when Savannah takes a seat at the breakfast bar next to me and crunches her teeth through a pickle I feel my stomach roll.

"Excuse me." I quickly rush out the kitchen before I throw up. Leia's sister kindly directs me to the bathroom and I only just make it to the toilet before I spew.

"Shit." I roll my eyes. I knew I was coming down with something, I've felt it coming on for a few days, and now I could have spread it to everyone here. I wait until I'm sure I'm done before standing up and patting some water on my face. Then I check my reflection before opening the door to head downstairs to ask for a lift home. I almost jump out of my skin when I see Savannah waiting on the other side of the door with a suspicious look on her face.

"You got something you want to share?" She crosses her arms over her stomach and tips her head to one side.

"I must be coming down with something, I thought it was just nerves building up, but—"

"Oh, come on, we both know what this is." She shakes her head and laughs. "Way to go, Mitch."

"Savannah, I don't know what you're talking about." I stare back at her.

"You're dizzy, you threw up because of my pickle. I know the signs." The smile on her face keeps getting wider.

"Wait, you think I'm...? Oh, no. I can't be."

"Believe me, here you *will* be. I swear they put something in the water."

"No, seriously. I can't... I can't have children. It was something that was done to me at the village." I feel the heavy weight of reality sink into my stomach.

"And you're sure?" Savannah frowns.

"Positive, I was pregnant once before and..." I tear up real quick because now's not the time to be talking about this, not in a home so full of love and happiness.

"So, answer me this, are you and Mitch being careful?" She still doesn't seem convinced.

"Savannah, you're not hearing me. We don't have to be careful because there is no chance of me getting pregnant. Solomon made sure of it."

"Come with me." She grabs my wrist and drags me down the stairs so fast I don't have time to protest.

"Me and Everleigh are running back to my place. I'm sure I borrowed the big pot last week," she calls through to the kitchen as she rushes us out the front door and toward her car.

"Where are we going?" I ask, getting into the passenger seat as she takes the wheel.

"To my place. I still have a bunch of tests left over. Cole made me take like twenty of the things before he believed me." She starts the engine and pulls off with a skid.

"I appreciate your help, but I know it can't be possible. Magna specialized in that kind of thing."

"Well, in that case, humor me." Savannah smiles as she pulls up outside her place and rushes us inside.

She marches me through the cabin to her bathroom and struggles down onto her knees to reach into the back of the cabinet and pull out a box.

"There, now get peeing." She uses the basin to steady herself back onto her feet.

"Well, can you at least turn around?" I laugh at her as I try reading the instructions.

"Here." She pops the cap off the end. "You pee on this bit. Then we wait for the two pink lines."

Turning her back to me, she hums as if it's gonna make this any less awkward, and realizing that I'm not gonna win this battle, I get on and do as she instructs.

"All done." I pop the cap back on and place the test on the side by the basin while I wash my hands. Is it mad that I feel a tiny niggle of hope, despite knowing that what Savannah is suggesting is impossible? It's so stupid of me to even think that way, maybe I should start seeing Samantha again. It's been a while.

"How long does it take?" I sit on the edge of the bath, feeling more and more foolish as the seconds tick by.

"Well, it should take another minute, but it doesn't need to too—" She holds the test out to me with a clever look on her face. "I told ya..."

I stare at the plastic stick that she's holding in front of me and when I see two very prominent pink lines I snatch it from her hand.

"You're very pregnant, they usually only show up faint in the early weeks. When was your last period?"

"I don't know, some time ago, I don't keep track of it. Savannah, this isn't possible." I look up at her, still in shock.

"It looks like it to me. No period, feeling sick, dizzy, *and* a positive test, the odds are stacked up. Welcome to the club."

She slides her hand over her stretched-out stomach and suddenly I feel very sick again.

I'm happy. Of course, I'm happy, this is something I never even let myself imagine could happen. But I have no idea how Mitch is going to feel. It was hard enough for me to convince him that he and I were a good idea, and now a baby.

"Don't look so scared, this is gonna be awesome." Savannah smiles before lifting the toilet lid back up for me to spew.

"This part, not so much, but you know what I mean." She strokes my back for me as I hurl some more.

CHAPTER 33

HUNTER

"Little fucker's gotten away," Tate yells as he trots up beside me. "Someone's gonna have to go after him, he's running in the opposite direction to the herd."

"I got it." I look across at Mitch who is busy holding the left side.

"Ya sure?" he checks, pulling the bandana down from the lower half of his face. These cattle are sure as hell kicking up some dust.

"Everyone else is needed here. I can rope him, I've been practicin'," I assure him, still feeling that bitter disappointment that he's not who I thought he was. I was getting used to the idea of this being my life. Now, I'm not so sure, it just kinda feels like I'm stealing someone else's.

"Get goin' then." He winks at me, before covering the bottom half of his face back up.

I kick on Blaze and head in the same direction as the steer that got away, he's got some distance on me and is moving fast, but the treeline he just ran into should slow him down. It'll just make finding him that much harder. I follow him into the small woodland that separates Grid 6 and 7, then pull Blaze to a halt when I see a woman knelt by the stream collecting water.

"You okay, ma'am?" I ask, wondering what the hell she's doing out here in the ass-end of nowhere. She's dressed all kinds of weird and has far too many layers on for the heat.

"Oh, I'm fine." She stands up and when she turns around and looks up at me, both our faces drop in shock.

"Mom?" I squint my eyes, unable to believe that it's her. Sure, she's a little older than the girl in the picture, but just like Everleigh said, she's aged well. I'm undoubtedly looking at my mother.

"You have to leave," she whispers, rushing toward me when I jump off Blaze's back.

"What are you doing here, did you come here to find me?" I ask, feeling some hope.

"No. I mean yes. He did, but you have to leave, you can't be part of this."

She looks scared and desperate, and it makes me even more curious as to what's going on here.

"Leave? Mom, I've been trying to find you. I looked everywhere. I tried your sister and—"

"I know, how do you think he found you?" She reaches up her hand and slides it over my stubbly jaw. "You're so handsome." She smiles proudly, as tears well in her eyes. "You're in danger, Hunter, get on this horse and ride away from here."

"Are you crazy? I've been looking for you for years, I'm not riding away from ya now. And who do I need to be afraid of?" I shake my head in confusion. Nothing she's saying is making any sense. Her eyes are wild and fearful and when I reach out to take her hand in mine, she shakes her head.

"No, please." I can see her focusing on something past my shoulder and when I turn around to see what it is, I'm too late. The heavy weight smashes against the back of my skull and I feel the thud as I drop to the ground.

I wake up with my head thumping, surrounded by darkness. My wrists are bound and so are my ankles, and it's so stuffy in here that I choke.

"Help!" I scream out, trying to piece together what just happened. Did I really see my mom here at Copper Ridge, or was it something that my mind thought up while I was out cold? "Can someone help?" I call, fidgeting against the ropes and trying to find a way to get free.

The door eventually opens and I look up at the tall, large man that towers over me.

"Keep the noise down, boy," he warns.

"How about untie me?" I stare up at him, wondering who the hell he is. He's dressed the same kinda way she was, in a loose white shirt with suspenders on.

"I can't do that, not until I know I can trust you." He takes a seat on one of the crates in the corner and keeps his eyes focused on me.

"Where's Everleigh?" he growls at me.

"What do you want with her?" I narrow my eyes at him. I may not know Everleigh all that well, but she's sweet-natured and only just healing from everything she's suffered. That, and the fact that Mitch is clearly in love with her makes me feel the urge to protect her.

"She's to join us on our journey and we must leave soon. But first, I need to know I can trust you."

"Trust me? You got me tied up," I point out to him.

"Everything my father built was destroyed, but I am the resurrection. The Lord speaks to me now and I'm leading this family on a new path."

"I want to speak to my mom," I tell him, I know now that it *was* real. This asshole in front of me is clearly from the cult

Everleigh was rescued from and now I know they're here to take her on this *journey*, I need to enlist some help.

"You will in good time, but I can't have you fight me on this, Hunter. My father was wrong in having you sent away. You have always belonged with us, and I want you to be part of our uprising. There is a settlement across the border, one that will welcome us. They need men, strong men like me and you. You can take wives of your own."

"What?" I shake my head at him wondering if I'm hearing him right. "I don't want a wife. I'm happy here and so is Everleigh, so you can make your *journey* to the promised land by yourself."

"No." He stands up. "You must follow your true path. You're coming with us." Storming out, he slams the door behind him and I press my head back against the wall, trying to think of a way out of this.

I need to get a warning to Mitch, this guy is here for Everleigh and right now all the women are back at the ranch, unprotected. There's barely any light in here but I shift myself about and feel around for something that might help free me. I have no idea where I am or how far away the ranch is, but I have to try and do something.

The door opens again and this time the woman who I saw down by the stream steps inside.

"Hunter." Mom smiles as she kneels on the floor in front of me.

"What's going on? Is he holding you too? Forcing you to go with him to that place?" I ask her

"No, I belong to Solomon now, he's my husband." The smile is still fixed on her face as if that's a good thing.

"Mom, none of this is right, you have to let me go. I have to get some help for Everleigh. She's happy here."

"He's already left to get her. Today's his best chance, he's been watching, he knows that all the men are away from the big house so he's going to find out where he can find Everleigh, from the women they left behind." I can tell from the guilt on her face that she knows this is wrong. I also know that Everleigh is at the ranch. I just don't know what lengths that man will go to, to get her.

"Mom, you can't let this happen, you have to untie me. Let me help her," I beg, hoping she can see how wrong all this is.

"I never wanted to give you away." She slides her hand through my hair and smiles sadly. "I pleaded and prayed that I could keep you."

"Then why didn't you?"

"I was a pastor's daughter, being pregnant so young and without a husband was never going to be allowed. Not in our culture."

"Our culture?" I shake my head trying to understand what that culture is.

"My father had been raised in the village, he left when he met my mom and they moved here to Fork River to make a life for themselves. They had me, and then your aunt, and everything was fine. Until..." She pauses and shakes her head.

"Until you got pregnant with me," I finish for her.

"I don't regret having you, Hunter, even when they took you away from me, I didn't regret the time while you were growing inside me." She wipes away the tears that stream down her face. "Please, be a good boy and come with us."

"I'm not a child, anymore. I'm a man and I'm happy here. So is Everleigh. I won't let that asshole take her back to Hell."

"Hunter, please don't fight him."

"Why did you lie on my birth certificate? Why did you put Mitch as the father?" I may be smack bang in the center of a crisis here, but I have to know the answer.

"Because he's a good man, and I wanted my son to at least believe he came from that."

"Where did I come from? Who's my real father?" I plead with her to tell me. I want to feel like I belong again.

She looks down at her hands and shakes her head.

"I need you to tell me. I deserve to know where I came from. You lied and I want to know why." I can feel myself getting angry with her, which is not what I wanted to happen.

"Trust me, Hunter, you don't." She squeezes my hand so tight I can feel her shaking. "Mitch was the best option I could give you. As soon as my father found out I was pregnant, he packed us up and moved us out of town. Then he sent me away to the village. Abraham allowed me to keep you until I gave birth, and then we had to register you and sign off on the adoption. Abraham arranged for one of the men from the village to go to the courthouse with me and pretend to be the father. We needed a name and that's the first name I thought of." She smiles fondly before snapping herself out of it. " I didn't know what kind of family you'd end up with and I wanted peace of mind that, if you ever came looking for your real parents, you'd find something good."

"Well, you were right, Mitch *is* a good guy and right now you're letting that man who has me tied up, destroy his life," I point out, hoping it'll make her see some sense.

"I can't stop Solomon. No one can. He's our leader now, and God talks to him. This is what he wants. He wants us to be together." She forces a smile for me and I shake my head in disbelief.

"I'm not coming with you and neither is Everleigh. And you are gonna tell me right now who my father is," I tell her sternly. I'm losing my patience because time is running out and I'm tied up here, helpless.

"Please, Hunter." She closes her eyes and shakes her head.

"Mom, I deserve to know where I really came from."

"You came from evil." She opens her eyes and stares right through me. "Pure, damned evil," she repeats. "The man who put you inside me took me without my permission. He forced me." Her confession stuns me silent and makes my stomach clench.

"Who?" Is all I can focus on, when I see the pain in her eyes.

"He owned a ranch close to here that I took a summer job at. Your father is Ronnie Mason and a man that I never wanted you to ever come to know."

"Ronnie Mason." I recall hearing that name before, his sister is the person who sent Garrett that head.

"He's dead," I say my thoughts out loud. "His sister moved into his house, she's causing shit for the Carsons." That's as much as I know, though the severed head tells me there's a lot more to it.

"Hunter, this is our chance to make up for all that lost time. Abraham wouldn't accept you, but Solomon will. You have to let him know that he can trust you. We can be together."

"We could be together here," I tell her. "The Carsons are good people. I have a job, I can take care of us. Help me get loose, let me help Everleigh. You know Solomon, and the people he wants to take us to, are bad."

"Not as bad as he was." She shrugs. "My father blamed me, said I made myself a temptation. I swear that's not what I wanted from him." She starts to cry again, and being bound so tight means I can't comfort her.

"I have to go. We need to prepare for the journey." She suddenly stands up and wipes her eyes again.

"Mom, don't," I beg her one last time.

"Don't fight him, Hunter, my heart would break if you got

hurt." She turns her back on me and walks out, ignoring me when I scream for her to come back.

"I don't want anyone to know, yet." I reach out and stop Savannah from getting out of the car when we pull back up outside the ranch. "Not until I've seen a doctor and made sure, or until I've spoken to Mitch." I'm still in complete shock. I thought becoming pregnant was impossible, I'd resided myself to the idea of never being a mother, and now this. It's so overwhelming that I can't think straight.

"Our secret." Savannah draws a zip over her mouth before getting out the car and leading us inside. The house is full of chaos just like we left it and when I see Leia holding baby Dalton on the couch and feeding him from one of her breasts, I allow myself to imagine how wonderful it would feel to do that to my own child.

"No luck with the big pot?" Maddy steps into the room looking flustered.

"No, we looked everywhere." Savannah shakes her head.

"It must be in the bunkhouse. I'm sure Josie made a chili in it for the boys the other day."

"I'll grab it," I call out, needing to get some air. I can't stop worrying about how Mitch is going to react to this. He constantly reminds me that he's too old for me, will he feel too old for this? Will he be mad, and disappointed? What if it changes the way he feels about me?

"You sure?" Maisie checks.

"Yeah, I'll head over there, right now." I fake a smile and try not to move too fast as I rush toward the door to get out of there. Once I'm on the porch I take in a long, deep inhale of air and place my hand over my stomach.

I still can't quite believe there's a child inside me, one that me and Mitch created together. And despite being unsure about how Mitch will react, I can't help feeling blessed by it. I let the smile remain on my face as I walk across the yard toward the bunkhouse, letting myself imagine how happy the three of us could be in our cozy little cabin.

I hear a bang over by the stable after I've passed it but when I stop and look back over my shoulder there's nothing there. I figure it must be one of the horses that got left behind and decide to continue to make my way toward the bunkhouse to find this big pot.

"I missed you, little dove." My breath gets stuck in my throat when I turn back around and see Solomon standing tall, in front of me.

It must be some illusion, he can't be here. Life wouldn't be that cruel.

"No." I shake my head and start backing away, but he reaches out and grabs my wrist, drawing me close to him.

"Shhhhh, don't panic. I won't hurt you." He wraps his arm around my middle, crushing me as he lifts me off the floor and when he starts carrying me toward an old RV that's parked under the trees, on the other side of the gate, I go to scream so I can alert the girls. His hand slams over my mouth and the fight I put up seems useless against his huge frame. Still, I don't give up. I can't go back.

He throws me into the back of the van, grabbing some rope

and looping it around my wrists so he can tie me to the handle of one of the cupboards.

"Please, don't do this, Solomon, *Please.*"

"You belong to me, little dove. You didn't think I'd let you get away, did you?" He smiles as he slams the door and then a few seconds later I hear him start the engine. My bones rattle as he drives at speed over the rough terrain, taking me further and further away from the Carson ranch. I scream at him, begging him to take me back, but all I see is the back of his head and all I hear is him whistling that song that always warned me he was on his way to me.

I scream until my throat feels like it's bleeding and still he ignores me until he pulls to a stop. I wait for him to get out and for the door to open before I slam my foot hard into his chest. But it makes no difference, he still comes at me, untying my arms and having no consideration for me, or the child I'm carrying, as he drags me across the ground toward a tiny outbuilding. During my struggle, I catch glimpses of my surroundings and I swear I see Annie holding a small child. I scream at her for help but nothing comes of it, and when Solomon opens the door to a rickety, old outhouse and tosses me inside, he grips both my wrists and forces them over my head. He tethers me with more rope to whatever's behind me.

"What are you doing with her?" A voice I recognize comes from behind him and when I try to look around his legs, I scream when his palm stings my cheek.

"Stay still, girl," he growls at me as he checks his knots are tight enough and causes my pulse to beat fast against the ropes.

"Solomon?" Annie comes rushing to the door, looking at me guiltily.

"Help Kayla pack up the van! We have to leave before they realize these are gone," he yells back at her.

"But we're not ready. Solomon, you promised I could get Samuel his medicine."

"We'll get it in the next town, God blessed us with an opportunity today. It was no coincidence that Hunter was riding in the woods near here, alone, or that Everleigh was right there at the ranch when I went there to find out where she was. This was God's plan and we must adapt to it." He forces her out of the door and follows her out, slamming it behind him.

"Hunter." I look across and see him tied up the same as I am.

"Fuck, Everleigh. I tried to stop him. Are you hurt?" He looks worried.

"A little, I'm so scared." I try to breathe but I can feel my chest tightening with panic. I can't go back to what I came from, not now that I know life can be so good. It's dark and dingy here, just like it was in the bunker.

"Everleigh, you need to breathe, you're starting to panic."

"I'm pregnant." The words blurt out as I try to suck more air into my lungs. And I can see by the shock on Hunter's face that, me telling him that, has only made him become more fearful.

"That's great news." He manages to force a smile for me. "Does Mitch know?" He keeps smiling, trying to be encouraging, but it's not gonna work. I know how much danger we're in.

"I only just found out myself." I shake my head in response. "I didn't think I could and now—"

"Hey, hey. Don't you worry, now. I'm gonna get us outta here and then you can tell Mitch that he really does get to be a dad. He's gonna like that a whole lot." He tries to sound excited as his eyes dart around us, trying to find something to help. "I just need you to stay calm and remember to breathe. Don't go passing out on me, now." He smiles some more as I nod my head and agree.

"I can't go back there, Hunter." I feel the tears sliding down my cheeks.

"I know, and you won't have to, I promise. I'll do whatever it takes. Okay?"

"Okay," I whisper back at him, trying my best to act like I have faith in him.

The door opens back up a few minutes later and when Hunter's mother comes inside, I have to do a double take. "Kayla?" I stare at her wondering how she got here too. Is she working with Solomon to take me back?

"Annie has let the air out of one of the tires to buy us some time," she whispers. "Solomon's changing the wheel now." She goes to start untying Hunter, but he insists that she unties me, and when she eventually agrees she suddenly freezes when she hears her name called.

"Mom, come on," Hunter begs her.

"He'll kill you. He has a gun and if you try to run..." She shakes her head helplessly.

"Then you go back out there, and you tell him you're going to get water and you take my horse. You head out the trees toward that big ridge until you see the ranch and you get help," Hunter instructs her.

"I can't, I haven't ridden a horse since..."

"You can, and you will, because I'm your son, and Everleigh here, she's gonna have a baby, and look, she's really scared. Mom, I need you to do this for us," Hunter pleads with her. "Just be calm, don't act suspicious, and once you get to the ranch you stay there. It's safe."

Kayla nods her head as she stands up and when the door swings open and Solomon steps inside she screams when he grabs her by her hair.

"What are you doing?" His spittle lands on the side of her face when he talks.

"I was just checking they were ready to leave. We're going to need extra water, you don't want him looking ill when we show up at the new settlement." She smiles convincingly.

"Well, don't just stand there, go get it," Solomon tells her, turning her around and shoving her out the door.

"Everleigh." He crouches down in front of me and slides his hands up my leg. "I don't like how they dress you here." He turns his nose up at my jeans and unties the bottom of Mitch's shirt that I'm wearing over the top of my tee. "It shows off too much of what's mine." His fingers creep around my waist and make my stomach roll. He pulls my body closer to his and makes sure our lips are almost touching.

"You get the *fuck* away from her!" Hunter yells at him, and Solomon laughs a cruel, demonic laugh.

"We will be reacquainted soon, little dove." His palm slides between my legs, cupping my pussy and squeezing until I can't hold in the gasp of fear I make.

"I said, get your fucking hands off her, you bastard!" Hunter screams.

Solomon spins around and lands a punch on Hunter's jaw, then boots him in the stomach over and over until he's a groaning mess on the floor.

"You're gonna have to learn to hold your tongue where we're going, boy," he warns before heading out the door and slamming it shut.

"Hunter. Hunter. Are you okay?" I wait for him to respond with my heart beating fast.

"I'm fine." He chokes, as he manages to roll himself back up into a sitting position.

"Mom will help us. I know she will," he assures me, still

doing his best to stop me from panicking. But it's too late, my head is spinning and I can't see any way out of this mess.

"Someone should go looking for Hunter before it gets dark," I point out as we all trot through the gates to the ranch. It's strange that the girls ain't waiting out on the porch like they usually are and Garrett must notice too because he slides straight off his horse and hands his reins to Tate.

I do the same, following him across the yard and into the house, and as soon as I see Maisie pacing in front of the fire, I know something's wrong.

"What's happened?" Garrett goes straight to her, taking the tops of her arms in his hands and holding her still, while my eyes scan the room looking for Everleigh. There's no sign of her and when Wade and Cole both rush in behind me and go to their women, I really start to wonder where the fuck mine is.

"Where's Everleigh?" My voice comes out husky. I know it's her that's the problem because they all look at me, guiltily.

"We don't know, she left to get a pot from the bunkhouse about half an hour ago and she hasn't come back yet." Maisie shakes her head looking concerned.

"Well, have you looked for her?" I stare between all three of the girls.

"Of course, we have." Savannah uses Cole's forearm to get

herself up from the couch. "I searched the bunkhouse and the stables and Josie tried your cabin. She just called and said she's not there either."

"Then where the fuck is she?" I can feel my anger starting to take over, especially since we're rapidly losing daylight.

"Come on, Mitch, she can't have gone far, you know how nervous she is." Wade tries to calm me down, but it doesn't fuckin' work.

"Maybe she just wanted some space." Savannah shrugs, and the look on her face tells me she knows way more than what she's letting on.

"Did somethin' happen? Was she triggered by somethin'?" Garrett checks, and while Maisie and Leia shake their heads, Savannah bites her lip like she's holding something back.

"Savannah." Cole must notice too because he's giving her a look of warning.

She smiles at her husband, sweetly, but he shakes his head back at her. "Savannah, if you know somethin' ya have to tell us. It's gettin' dark out there," he points out sternly.

"I can't. I promised I wouldn't." She shakes her head defiantly and I'm just about to lose my shit when Maisie quickly intervenes.

"Savannah, this isn't the time to be worried about something like that. If what you know might help us find Everleigh you have to share it. For all you know, she could be lost and scared."

"Fine." Savannah blows out a frustrated breath as her eyes stare across the room and settle on mine.

"She's pregnant," she tells me, and of all the words I was expecting to hear, none of them were those.

"It's impossible." I shake my head.

"That's what she said but it's true, she was feeling sick and I picked up on it so I took her to our cabin and she did a test.

She's pregnant. She was overwhelmed by it all and she probably went to get the pot so she could get her head around the idea. She won't have gone far." Savannah looks at her husband and smiles awkwardly as all the rest of the heads in the room turn to me.

"I gotta find her." I storm out the door ready to get back on my horse and scan every fuckin' acre of this ranch. I don't know how what Savannah is claiming can be true, but I do know that Everleigh is vulnerable, and a night outdoors ain't safe.

"We're comin' with ya," Garrett says, as all three Carson men follow me out. "We'll send the boys back out too, each of us can cover a grid. We'll find her." I feel his hand slap my shoulder.

"Who the fuck is that?" I quickly turn my head when Cole alerts us of something in the distance. Hunter's horse is galloping into the yard with a woman riding his saddle instead of him. Her eyes are wide and she practically collapses to the ground as she slides off the saddle.

"You have to help them. He's got them," she manages as Garrett tries to aid her back onto her feet.

"Who's got who?" I take her by the shoulders and try to shake the answers out of her.

"Solomon, he came here for Hunter, and now he's got her too." She's breathless and her words come out shaky but they still fill me with dread.

"Naomi?" I look at the woman a little deeper in her eyes and recall the girl I once knew. The nod of her head confirms I'm right but we ain't got no time for a reunion.

"Where are they?" I squeeze her tight, desperate for answers.

"He's found a new place, he wants to take us all there but they don't want to go with him. She's so scared." I feel my heart actually stop beating when I think of how terrified she must be. I made Everleigh a promise, and I've failed her.

"Where are they?" I keep a firm grip on her, trying to keep her focused.

"Back that way." She looks over her shoulder. "He has an RV, it's old but it—"

"That son of a bitch. Grid 7!" I call out to anyone who can hear me, before hopping up onto Hunter's horse and taking the reins.

"He's got a gun," she warns me as I steer him to turn around.

"Mitch, wait for us to saddle back up." Garrett looks up at me.

"No time." I shake my head. "You wouldn't be hangin' around if that was your girl in trouble." I dig my heels into Blaze and take off, pushing him to his limits as I canter out the yard and head to Grid 7.

"Focus on me." Hunter does his best to keep me calm, but I can see how scared he is too. "You thought of any names for the kid?" he questions, acting as if we're not tied up about to be taken God knows where by a psychopath.

I shake my head and focus on finding my next breath, "Well, I'm just putting it out there, Hunter's a pretty solid name." He smiles nervously and as much as I appreciate his attempts to distract me, they are ineffective. I know how Solomon works, he always gets his way and if help doesn't hurry up and get here, I'll never see Mitch again. I can't even think about the child I have growing inside me right now, if I do I know I'll lose my head completely.

The door swings open and Solomon trudges inside, taking the rope that binds me and slicing a knife through it. He snatches his hand around my wrist and starts to drag me outside, and all I hear is Hunter yelling at him to leave me alone.

I keep my eyes firmly closed, too scared to face up to what will happen next, and that's when I hear the sound of hooves thundering into the ground. I wonder at first if it's my heart beating out of my chest from fear, but when Solomon stops dead and turns around I allow myself to open my eyes and see Mitch galloping toward us.

"*Get your fuckin' hands off her!*" He dismounts the horse and comes toward us, but Solomon doesn't listen. Instead, he forces my body in front of him, then takes the knife he's holding in his other hand and presses the blade tight to my throat.

"She's mine," he tells Mitch with his hands trembling, and I see the fear in Mitch's eyes as he takes a step back and holds up his hands, defensively.

"Put the knife down so we can talk." His glance keeps shifting between the blade and my eyes and when I swallow, I feel it cut into my throat.

"You don't wanna hurt her, Solomon." Mitch shakes his head.

"But I will if I have to. She belongs to me and no one else. Do you think it's a coincidence that I came here looking for the boy and found her in the *same* town? That's God's work." He laughs hysterically.

"You're scarin' her, look," Mitch gestures his head toward me, trying to play on Solomon's empathy. But he won't find any, I learned that very fast when I was down in that bunker at his mercy.

"Solomon, I'm gonna ask you politely one more time to put that knife down."

"And if I don't?" Solomon challenges him.

"Well, then things are gonna get real messy." I've never seen Mitch look more threatening.

"I won't let you have her. I told you, she's mine."

"Everleigh, darlin'," Mitch is focused on me now, acting like Solomon isn't even there. "Don't be scared, this man ain't gonna hurt you," he promises.

"How can you be so sure?" Solomon's hand tenses.

"Because if God truly wanted ya to have her, He wouldn't

have told you to kill her. You're not livin' in your village, anymore. You can't manipulate people with your lies and your deceit. If it was God's voice you were hearin', He wouldn't be tellin' ya to slit the throat of this sweet, innocent girl." I feel Solomon loosen his grip on me.

"Don't hide behind the façade anymore, Solomon, it's time to stand up and be a man. You want her, *I* want her. You're in the real world, now, and there's only one way for two men to settle a disagreement." Mitch slowly starts to unbutton his cuffs and rolls the sleeves of his shirt up to his elbows.

"You want me to fight you?" Solomon laughs as if the concept confuses him.

"What's the matter? Ain't ya ever had to fight for somethin' before?" Mitch appears to be waiting patiently while Solomon thinks it over, but I see the fear glistening in his eyes as he stares t into mine.

"Come on, Solomon, ya got me on age, and you're a big guy. If I were you, I'd be likin' my chances." Mitch cracks his knuckles and I feel the blade move a little further away from my skin.

"You wanna watch me kill him, little dove?" he whispers into my ear before he kisses my cheek, and I watch Mitch's jaw tense with fury.

I hear the sound of a baby crying but I can't turn my head. I'm too afraid.

"Don't go anywhere. I have plans for us." He shoves me to the side, and I breathe a long sigh of relief until he lunges forward and tries to stab Mitch with the knife.

"No!" I scream as Mitch manages to dodge him, getting a good hit on his face in the process. It still doesn't change the fact that Solomon is armed and Mitch isn't. I can hear a whole lot of commotion up ahead and when I look up and see men on horses in the distance, I pray that they hurry.

Solomon shows he has no fighting skills by constantly hacking the knife in Mitch's direction and when Mitch manages to get a hold of his wrist, he twists it back around his body at an angle so awkward, that Solomon falls to his knees and drops it from his hand. I watch as Mitch kicks him in his back sending the top half of his body, and his face, into the dirt. Then picking up the knife in one hand, he lifts Solomon's head up by his hair and draws him back up onto his knees. Now, Mitch is the one with the blade in his hand and he's holding it against Solomon's throat.

"You won't let him kill me." He looks up at me as if I'm the one who can save him. "You're good, Everleigh, and I was good to you, remember?"

"Look away, sweetheart," Mitch tells me in that soft voice that always soothes me.

"Everleigh, God will never forgive you if you let him kill me," Solomon speaks up again, the fear in his voice getting more and more desperate.

"You're right." I step closer and take the blade from Mitch's hand. He looks confused as he keeps a firm hold on Solomon, then just as he's about to say something, I interrupt him.

"He'd much prefer if I did it myself." I think about the baby that he had ripped from my womb as I slice the blade across his throat and watch the blood spill from the gash I've made. His eyes bulge with shock before Mitch releases him, and as I watch him turn pale and convulse on the floor, I drop the bloody knife from my hand and allow Mitch to scoop me up in his arms.

"Everleigh." His lips press into the top of my head as he squeezes me so tight I can barely breathe, but I don't care. I like how it feels, and I stop pretending to be brave and burst into tears.

"We have to help Hunter," I whisper, staring at the body that's now still.

"Is he hurt?" Mitch pulls himself away to check me over properly. "Are you hurt, what about the bab—"

"You know?" I stare at him in shock.

"Savannah had to tell us." I wish I could read from his face how he feels about it, but he's giving nothing away.

"I'm sorry, I thought it was impossible." I shake my head.

"Sorry... What the hell ya sorry for?" He laughs as the sound of hooves gets closer.

"Well, I'm assuming having kids wasn't on your agenda and we weren't careful because of what I told you. I swear, I'm just as shocked as you are."

"You're damn right, havin' kids wasn't on my agenda. But we're havin' one." He smiles and looks down to where his hand is now resting on my stomach. "And I couldn't be happier about it." His eyes flick back up to mine.

Our moment is totally ruined by five men on horses who immediately jump off their saddles and stare at the body on the floor.

"Looks like you had it covered, old man." Finn slaps him on the shoulder.

"Actually, Everleigh killed him," he tells them with a proud grin on his face. Right now, I feel no remorse for taking the life of a man who played such a big role in ruining mine, but we'll see how I feel when the adrenaline wears off.

"Good work." Finn nods his head as if I've impressed him.

"Get this piece of shit off our land," Garrett orders, and just as Finn and Tate set to work, we hear a feeble voice come from the outhouse.

"Any chance someone could untie me."

"I forgot about him." Mitch kisses me before he makes his way over to free Hunter, and when I hear the sound of the baby again, I turn around and see Annie standing at the door of the RV. She stares at the ground where Solomon is lying and bursts into tears like she's saddened by it.

"Annie, I'm sorry." I step closer so I can comfort her.

"Is it over?" she whispers, sounding as if she's too scared to believe it's true.

"He's dead," I confirm, feeling her make that same long sigh of relief that I did. It's enough to tell me that she's suffered too and that she's grateful to be free.

"He took me and Kayla when the village got raided. Told us we belonged to him. It's been hard." She closes her eyes and when tears streak out the sides of her cheeks, I hug her and her little boy, a little tighter.

"I need to get him some help, he's been sick for days," she informs me.

"Well, you're in luck, we just so happen to be headin' for a hospital," Mitch cuts in, dusting off his hands as he comes out of the outhouse, followed by Hunter. Hunter looks a little worse for wear from the beating he took but I can tell from the smile on his face when he sees me, that he's okay.

"C'mon, let's go get you and our baby checked out." Mitch slides his arm around my waist.

"I'm fine, I don't need a hospital." I shake my head because just the thought of being back in one freaks me out.

"Darlin', you've been through an ordeal, and we need to check everythin's okay. I'll be right there with ya. I won't let anyone do anythin' you don't want. You're in control," he promises.

"You good to ride?" He looks to Hunter, who nods his head.

"Good, ride on back to the ranch, there's someone there who's keen to talk to ya. I'll drive this RV back to my place with the girls, so Everleigh can shower and change, then I'll take 'em to the hospital.

I look down at my tee and see that it's covered in Solomon's blood. Mitch is right, we can't go anywhere with me looking like this.

"What will you tell them?" I ask, already starting to panic. I have nothing but bad memories associated with hospitals and if they knew what happened here, surely there would be an investigation.

"We'll just tell 'em that ya took a little tumble and I'm bein' over-cautious." Mitch calms me when he strokes my face. "Come on, get in." He opens the door to the RV for me and Annie to get inside.

I sit on the chair beside the bed and watch the nurse prod and poke Everleigh, all the while her eyes remain tightly shut and her hand squeezes mine.

"Well, it looks as if the fall didn't harm you, there's no tenderness. And the baby has lots of protection in there." Her smile is warm and reassuring, though Everleigh doesn't see it because her eyes are still closed.

"I don't even know if I'm pregnant, the test said I was but I can't..." She shakes her head and breathes slowly.

"Tests are rarely wrong, but we can take a look if you'd like peace of mind."

"Yeah, we want that." I jump in. Needing to know for sure that they're both okay.

"Sure, I'll go find a sonogram machine, just try to relax." She leaves us alone and Everleigh still keeps her eyes shut.

"Darlin', you can open your eyes, I'm here, and everythin's okay."

"I can't. I hate these places, the lights are too bright and it reminds me of those first few days I was free. Everything was so loud and chaotic. It was too much. I was so scared they'd never let me go."

"Well, you're free now, and you're safe." I kiss her hand and wait for the nurse to return.

"Everleigh, do you remember how long ago your last period was? It will help me determine whether to examine you externally or internally."

"Externally," I answer for her, knowing that an internal examination would be too much for her. "She's, erm, she's suffered some trauma in the past," I explain, hearing my voice go weak when I think about how close she came to suffering it again.

"No problem, early pregnancy can be hard to detect that way, but we'll do our best." I watch her prepare the machine until she asks me to dim the lights.

"This might feel a bit cold," she warns Everleigh before squirting some gel on her stomach. I take her hand again, to let her know I'm right with her as the nurse presses the wand that's attached to the machine, against her lower stomach.

"The lights are low, you can open your eyes," I whisper. But Everleigh shakes her head. The nurse is taking her time and I'm starting to wonder myself if that test was wrong, but then a sound fills the room that makes it undeniable.

"Is that?"

"That is the heartbeat of a very, healthy baby," she confirms, twisting the screen around so I can see for myself. I squint to see what she's pointing at, but it soon becomes very clear.

"Everleigh, open your eyes," I encourage her. "You *really* need to see this." I turn my attention to her, wanting to see her reaction. "Please, trust me, you don't wanna miss this." Eventually, she opens them and when she sees the image on the screen she bursts into happy tears.

"Is that really our baby?" She covers her mouth, laughing and crying all at the same time.

"It sure is, I'd say you're about seven weeks along from the measurements. Congratulations." The nurse leaves the image on the screen as she puts the wand back in its place and hands Everleigh some tissue.

"But I was told I couldn't have kids. They... She made it so I couldn't." Everleigh speaks up and the nurse looks confused.

"Were you told that by a medical practitioner?" she asks, with a frown.

"No."

"Well, I've been doing this for a long time and I can assure you that you are one hundred percent pregnant." The nurse smiles again.

"She's sure." Everleigh looks at me and bursts into tears again, and I take her face in my hands and kiss her, trying to think of a time in my life when I've been this happy.

"Come on, let's get ya home."

"What about Annie?" she asks, suddenly looking panicked again.

"I texted Garrett, he's makin' sure she and her kid have a room at the guest house, Cole and Maisie are waitin' with her down in pediatrics," I assure her.

"Here's some information you need about the do's and don'ts. I've also written you a prescription for some prenatal vitamins. You'll need to make a follow-up appointment with your local midwife in a few weeks, to check on baby's development." She opens the door for us and sees us out.

Taking Everleigh's hand, I lead us out the hospital, feeling like the luckiest man on the planet.

Everleigh's lying out on the couch fast asleep, what happened today has really taken its toll on her, and I'm so relieved that she's resting. I sit beside her with her legs resting on my lap and my hand splayed over her flat stomach. I'm gonna be a dad, I still haven't let it sink in completely because it feels too good to be true. I'm scared as hell, but she'll never know it. Being scared only proves how important it is to me to get this right and from now on all this girl will ever know is happiness.

Everleigh is gonna be the most perfect mother, and yeah, I'm gonna be a little older and stiffer than the other dads in the schoolyard, but I'm gonna take this life I've been blessed with by the balls and enjoy every second of it.

A knock at the door interrupts my thoughts and I'm careful not to disturb her as I get up and make my way over to answer it.

"Hunter." I smile at him as I let him in, heading straight for the cupboard where I keep the good stuff and grabbing two glasses.

"She okay?" He looks over the top of the couch, looking pleased to see her sleeping.

"Yeah, thanks to you." I hand him a good measure of scotch and clink my glass against his.

"I didn't do nothin'." He shakes his head and takes a seat at the table.

"You convinced your mom to come and let us know where ya were, and you kept her from freakin' out when you two were locked in that store buildin'. I owe ya, kid."

"Ronnie Mason's my father," he blurts the words out, and I knock back what I've got left of my drink and pour myself another.

"Did ya hear what I said?" he asks when I remain silent.

"Aye, I heard ya." I nod my head and keep my eyes focused on the liquid in my glass.

"He raped her." Hunter keeps his voice low and when I

look up and see the anger on his face, I pour him another drink too.

"I can't stay here, the Carson's hate the Mason family."

"You ain't a Mason!" I hiss through my teeth, feeling the anger building inside me too.

"We can pretend, but it ain't gonna change the truth, and there is no way I'm gonna be accepted here once the others find out."

"Hunter, there was a man who raised you for twenty-five years before you came here. A man who loved you. Ronnie Mason is not your *fuckin' father,*" I remind him.

"I lied." He hangs his head looking ashamed of himself. "I didn't have a good upbringing before I came here, at all. My adoptive mom tried to be good to me but my father hated me. They thought it was me that knocked up that girl from my school because we were close, and my dad used it as an excuse to be rid of me as soon as he could. He kicked me out of home the day after I graduated and my mom just stood back and let him. I've been sleeping rough ever since."

"Hunter." I shake my head, wondering why the hell he felt the need to lie to me. "Why didn't you just be honest with me?"

"I didn't want you to think I was the poor, broken kid that came lookin' for his real dad because I was all out of options. It wasn't like that. And when I learned about you, and spent time around this place, for the first time in my life I felt like I belonged somewhere. Now, this...." He cracks his knuckles and tenses his jaw.

"It makes no difference that Mason's your father, Hunter, how many times do I have to tell you that?"

"But he *is* my blood. And what he did to her..." He knocks back his drink so he doesn't have to say it. "What if one day, I turn out just like him?" All the anger in his eyes turns to fear and I can't help feeling sorry for the kid.

"Ya won't, you're a good person, I knew that from the second I met ya and you proved it today when you took care of Everleigh. Mason may have been the one who knocked up your mom, but it's *my* name that's on your birth certificate. I'm holdin' myself fuckin' accountable for makin' sure you continue to be that good person," I tell him, and I mean every word. I've raised men who weren't my sons before, there's no reason for Hunter to be any different.

"You don't have to do that, I ain't a charity case."

"I know damn well I don't have to. I want to." I look him dead in the eye so he knows I mean it.

"A lotta things have happened lately that got me believin' in fate, and all those years ago when your mom named me as your father because she was all outta options, I believe she set a path for ya." I top our glasses and hold mine up. "Stick around, and I'll make a cowboy outta ya, Hunter Hudson."

The boy frowns at me like he's confused.

"Are you sayin'..."

"The name's on the certificate, if ya don't wanna keep your adoptive dad's name, I'd be proud for ya to take mine."

"Do you mean it?"

"Kid, you'll learn fast, that I never say *anythin'* I don't mean." I clink my glass against his when he smiles.

"Does this mean I get to take the bran—"

"No." I shut him down.

Two Months Later

"What ya doin'?" Mitch sneaks up behind me and rests his hands on my stomach. I'm definitely starting to show, and feeling much better now that the sickness has worn off.

"I'm writing a letter to my sister." I shock and please him at the same time. "I think she should know that she's getting a niece or a nephew, and I read her letter," I confess.

"When?" Mitch takes a seat beside me looking intrigued.

"When you were helping Hunter move Annie and Naomi into their new place yesterday. I just felt like it was time."

"You never told me." His brows knit together.

"Well, we had a lot going on after," I remind him, since I've taken the leap and let the Carsons in, there's been no going back. And I wouldn't have it any other way. I can't believe I spent so long hiding away from them. I like how it feels to be part of a family, it makes me even more excited for when our little one comes along.

"Ya still should have told me." He reaches across the table and kisses me.

"I wanted to get everything straight in my head before I

wrote this. I need to be strong for when the baby gets here and this is one of the final steps." I smile at him.

"Well, I'm very proud of ya." The smile on his face proves it.

"There's something else I need to do before I can move on." I stand up and head to the bedroom, taking my journal from the top drawer and standing in front of him.

"Samantha told me the best way to heal was to ease up some space in my head and speak out. I didn't want to face up to those memories, but I wanted so badly to heal so we could get closer. She suggested I write in this journal, she said once I had everything out, the control would be mine. I could decide what to do with those thoughts and memories after." I look down at the journal in my hands.

"I could keep this forever hidden in a drawer. I could burn it. But I want to share it with you." I lift my eyes up to his. "I need there to be someone in this world who understands me completely and I want that someone to be you. So, here." I hand it over to him, feeling fear and relief, all at once. "This is the first chapter of my story. The one that broke me and made me lose all faith in God and humanity."

"Everleigh." Mitch looks down at it with tears in his eyes.

"There will be parts that are hard to get past, but knowing the story has a happy ending will get you through." I smile at him through the happy tears that are blurring my eyes.

"I want to have a relationship with Addison, but I need to focus on our baby. I don't want to take any steps backward, and I'm explaining that to her in the letter. I hope she understands."

"She'll understand, she's just gonna be happy to hear from ya, darlin'." He takes me in his arms and pulls me close.

"Thank you," he whispers as his lips touch the top of my head.

"For what?" I pull away and laugh at him.

"For choosin' me to share this with, and for lettin' me be part of the next chapter."

"Well, I have a feeling the next chapter is gonna be interesting." I look down at the bump that's resting between us and smile. I've started to feel flutters these past few days, and it's the most incredible feeling in the world. I can't wait until Mitch can feel it too.

The door crashes open and when Leia bursts inside the excitement on her face tells me Savannah's suffering is finally over.

"Please tell me she's had it?" I sigh, knowing how uncomfortable and irritable Savannah's been getting since she passed her due date last week.

"Oh, she had it." Leia smiles. "And you won't believe where."

"Try us." Mitch wraps his arm around my neck and pulls my back tight against him.

"At the rodeo last night." Leia grins. "She never even made it to the hospital. She and Cole are at home with their little girl, right now. We just got back from visiting. I thought you might wanna be next."

"At the rodeo?" Mitch chuckles.

"I know, it's *so* Savannah." Leia rolls her eyes. "I gotta get back to the car, Dalton's due a feed, we'll see ya later."

"Thanks for letting us know," I call after her as she rushes back out the door, and when I look over my shoulder at Mitch and smile hopefully, he sighs.

"Come on, let's go meet her." He grabs his keys

———

Savannah doesn't look at all as if she's just given birth when we get to their cabin. She's in bed holding her little girl and looking as radiant as ever.

"Congratulations." I bend over to take a look at the new edition while Mitch shakes Cole's hand.

"How was it?" I ask nervously.

"Awful," Cole answers first. "It just happened so fast and then *boom*, she was here."

"You did a great job, honey." Savannah taps his arm sarcastically.

"It wasn't quite that fast, but honestly, it wasn't that bad. Once I calmed him down." She smiles at me and makes me feel a little better about what I have coming. "D'ya wanna hold her?" she asks.

"Of course, I do." I sit on the mattress beside her and let her place her precious, little bundle in my arms.

"Savannah, she's beautiful." I look down at her, noting how she has Savannah's chin and Cole's nose. I can't help wondering what features of us mine and Mitch's baby will have when they get here.

"You got a name for her yet?" Mitch asks, peering over my shoulder to take a look for himself.

"Still undecided." Cole looks at his wife and smiles

"Screw you, I pushed her into the world, so it's my choice. Her name's Evie," Savannah tells us.

"You told me you wanted Beyoncé." Cole looks stunned and very relieved.

"Baby, you should know by now that I like to keep you on your toes. You liked Evie and she looks like a little Evie. We can call the next one Beyoncé." She winks at me.

"That's beautiful." I stroke my finger over baby Evie's cheek.

There's a knock at the door and when Hunter steps through it, he loiters awkwardly with a bunch of flowers in his hand.

"Garrett said she'd arrived. These are for you." He passes them over to Savannah before scratching the back of his head.

"You want to hold her, Hunter?" Savannah offers.

"Oh no, no. You can't trust these hands with something as delicate as a baby." He laughs.

"He's right," Cole quickly intervenes.

"I just wanted to say congratulations and bring ya the flowers. I'm grateful to ya all for what you've done for me and Mom. I know we're not family, but you've sure as hell treated us like it." He smiles that awkward smile again before he backs up to leave.

"Hey, where ya goin'?" Cole calls him back.

"I figured you and your brothers will be celebrating so there'll be extra chores to do back at the ranch. I'll—"

"We're *all* gonna be celebratin'. You included." Cole makes his way around the bed and lifts his little girl out of my arms. "I want this little girl to have as many uncles, who know how to shoot straight, as she can get." He looks down at her lovingly.

"You don't have to be blood to be family, just loyal." He looks back up at Hunter who nods his head.

"Guess I better learn how to shoot straight then, huh?" The grin on his face makes us all laugh and after checking Savannah has everything she needs, we leave her to rest for a few hours before the homecoming party, for baby Evie, starts back at the ranch.

"Do you care what we have?" I ask Mitch as he drives us home.

"'Course I don't mind, whatever we have it'll be perfect." He reaches his hand across the console to pat my stomach proudly.

"Seeing her today just makes everything seem so real, we're

gonna have one of those soon." I slide my hand over his to keep it there. I love how it feels when Mitch touches me now, it's a comfort and I can't believe I spent so long fearing it.

"Trust me, it's real, so real that we're gonna have to extend the cabin. I spoke to the boys about it the other day, I reckon we can get somethin' fixed up before the baby comes."

"We have plenty of space." I laugh at him.

"And suppose I want him, or her, to have a brother or sister?" He looks over to me with a mischievous grin on his face.

"There was you saying you felt too old to date me, now you want us to have an army." I shake my head.

"Well, suddenly I'm feelin' very young again. I've got me a new lease of life," he tells me as we pull up outside our cabin. I've not even opened the door before he's around my side and helping me out.

"You got any other plans for our future?" I ask as I step up onto the porch.

"It just so happens I do." He shocks me when he drops down onto one knee and takes off his hat.

"I've been thinkin' of ways I can do this to make it special, but I can't wait any longer." He reaches into his pocket and pulls out a ring.

"Everleigh, you've changed my life, you've brought out a side of me that I never knew existed and I just have to have you as my wife." He looks up at me and waits for my answer, and I nod my head while I try to overcome all the emotions that have hit me at once. Tears stream down my face as he slides the ring onto my ringer and when he stands back up and kisses me and our baby stirs within me, this moment makes all the dark ones I had to endure suddenly feel worth the fight.

EPILOGUE

MITCH

Seven Months Later

"Mitch, wake up." I feel her shaking me "Mitch, it's time."

"I told ya, I'm not workin' today." I try and pull the covers back over us but she shakes me even harder.

"Mitch, the baby's coming."

My eyes shoot open and I sit up straight.

"Why the fuck didn't ya say somethin'?" I stand up and start pacing the floor.

"I was trying to." She laughs. She's in labor and she's laughing.

"What d'ya need?" I move closer to her, trying to remember what all those books we read together said, now it's all just fuzz in my brain.

"Relax, the contractions started a few hours ago."

"A few *hours*?" I check I'm hearing her right.

"Yes, but they were irregular and just uncomfortable. Now, they're starting to hurt." She grimaces as she grips hold of the nightstand.

"You havin' one now?" I look at her, feeling helpless, and when she nods her head all I can do is take her other hand and remind her to breathe.

"I think you should call the midwife now." She looks at me once it passes. "They're coming every five minutes. That's when she said to call."

"Okay. I can do that." I leap back off the bed and head for the kitchen where my cell phone is.

"Darlin'." I look back through the door. "You sure you wanna do it this way? At the hospital they have drugs and if anythin' goes wrong—"

"No hospitals." She shakes her head. "Stress is bad for the baby and if I go to a hospital I'll get scared. I'm much better off here where I feel comfortable."

I flick through my phone and dial the midwife, not at all liking the response I get when I speak to her.

"Shit!" I hang up the phone and breathe myself calm before I head back to the bedroom to break the news.

"Mitch, there's another one coming." She reaches her hand out to me and I take it, stroking her back and deciding to let it pass before I tell her what I know.

"It's over." She breathes a sigh of relief and smiles up at me. How the hell is this woman making being in labor look hot?

"Sweetheart, I just spoke to the midwife. She's on another delivery, right now." Her face instantly drops. "Now, ya don't need to worry, they can send us a replacement, but they might take a while to get here. Or, we could go to—"

"No hospitals," she tells me again, maneuvering herself up off the bed and pressing her palm into the arch of her back. "You can call the girls, they can help until the other midwife gets here." She starts to walk up and down the room, breathing calmly, and I quickly do as she says, calling Savannah and asking her to round the girls up and get here fast.

"They're on their way, is there anythin' I can do?"

"Just be here." She waddles over to me and I slide my hand gently over her huge, round stomach.

"Everythin's gonna be okay," I assure her, as nerves and excitement battle it out in my chest. And when Everleigh tenses to endure another contraction, the gush that hits the floor makes me jump back in shock.

"Oh, this is *definitely* happening." She winces.

"It sure is." I keep stroking her back and hope those girls hurry up and get here.

———

"That's good, Everleigh, it'll pass real soon." Maisie seems to know all the right things to say to her every time she gets a contraction. They're getting closer and closer together and lasting much longer, and I can see Everleigh's starting to get tired.

Savannah and Leia prepare the bed for the delivery by placing a waterproof sheet over the mattress, and I just stand holding Everleigh's hand, feeling like a spare part.

"I'm not ready." Everleigh suddenly starts shaking her head and starts to panic.

"What?" I look down at her on the chair she's perched on.

"This baby can't come yet. I'm not ready," she repeats, and Maisie looks up at me seeming just as confused as I am.

"Darlin', I don't think ya get a say in that, this baby's halfway to comin' and we're *more* than ready for it."

"No, I need us to be married." She shakes her head. "I know I said I wanted to wait till after the baby came but I've changed my mind. I want us to be married before it comes."

"Oh, sweetheart, it's too late for that, now. We can get married straight away, after. Tomorrow, if you want. Let's just focus on this, right now." I try and keep her calm.

"*Oh, fuck!*" She squeezes my hand as another contraction

hits her, and I breathe in sync with Maisie to help get her through it.

"I don't wanna have this baby until we're married, Mitch." She looks up at me helplessly, and I rack my brain trying to come up with a solution.

It's 7 am in the mornin'. Where the *fuck* am I gonna find a minister?

"Okay. I'll fix it." I grab hold of Maisie and drag her out the room.

"We need to get Garrett here," I tell her when we're in the kitchen out of earshot

"Garrett? He's gonna be even less useful than me." She looks at me as if I'm crazy.

"Not for that, you call him and tell him to have one of the boys sit with the triplets. We need him to come here and marry us, right now."

"Garrett can't marry you." She laughs at me.

"Sure he can, he's the town mayor he can do anythin' he wants." I pass her my phone because I have to get back to Everleigh.

"Mitch, being the mayor doesn't ordain him to marry people."

"Maybe not, but right now she doesn't need to know that. We got no midwife, a hospital is outta the question, and the last thing I wanna do is have her stressin'. Call your husband." I leave her to it and get back to Everleigh.

"Where did you go?" She tries getting into a more comfortable position on the chair we've bought in from the kitchen.

"To arrange a weddin'." I kiss her on her sweaty forehead and help her get settled.

"Well done, you're doin' great, she's makin' progress, right?" I look at Maisie. Wondering what the fuck is taking Garrett so long.

"How am I supposed to know?" she whispers back at me.

"Because you've given birth to three babies." I shake my head back at her.

"Giving birth does not qualify me as a midwife, you've probably got more experience in this than I have, you've birthed hundreds of calves.

"Mitch, there's another one coming already." Everleigh looks worried as she clutches my hand.

"She's got to be close to being fully dilated," Savannah points out.

"You're gonna have to check." Maisie looks at me.

"I'll get the gloves." Leia disappears into the kitchen.

"Maisie, this is very fuckin' different to deliverin' a calf, I know what I'm feelin' for."

"Mitch." Everleigh buries her head into my side and screams as another pain wracks through her body.

"Breathe, just breathe." I stroke her hair, and when Garrett rushes through the door I breathe a sigh of relief. He comes closer and screws up his face when he notices Everleigh doubled in pain.

"You sure she's up to this?" he checks.

"Yes, she's up to it!" Everleigh manages to growl at him, clutching at my shirt and nearly pulling it off my shoulders. "God, there's so much pressure I think I need to push," she sobs.

"I think we should get her to the bed." Maisie looks up at me and the urgency on her face has both me and Garrett helping Everleigh to her feet and moving her in that direction.

"What's with the Sunday best?" I notice what he's wearing

as we help her lay down. "Maisie said ya needed me to marry ya," he points out, looking serious, and I shake my head as I try to get Everleigh as comfortable as possible.

"*OHHHHHH!*" Everleigh clutches her stomach again, and Maisie lifts up her night dress to check what's happening.

"You better hurry up with those vows, minister." She looks up at her husband with a worried look on her face.

"Not a problem." Garrett clears his throat and pulls a Bible outta his jacket pocket.

"Where the hell did you find that?" I ask him.

"This just so happens to be the Carson family Bible, it's been in the family for decades,"

"Garrett." Maisie waves her hand at him, while Everleigh continues to breathe in through her nose and out through her mouth like Leia reminds her to.

"Dearly beloved, we are gathered here—"

"Cut the crap, we don't got time for it!" I yell at him as Everleigh crushes my hand tighter and starts to cry out in pain.

"You have to push, now," Maisie tells her, looking disturbed by whatever she's seeing down there.

"Right. Do you, Mitch Hudson, take this woman to be your lawfully, wedded wife? Do you promise to love, honor, and obey her as long as you both shall live?" he asks me.

"I do." I look Everleigh in the eyes and smile at her as I make my promise to her.

"And do you, Everleigh, I'm not quite sure of your second name, take this man to be your lawfully, wedded husband? To have and to hold, for rich or for poorer, for better or worse, and all that other stuff?" I look up at him and shrug, wondering where he's getting these words from. He's got his Bible open on Matthew 26:17 which, if I recall correctly, is the last *fuckin'* supper!

The face I get back from him tells me he's making this up as he goes along but now's not the time for me to be caring.

"I do." Everleigh manages.

"I can see the head, the baby's got hair." Maisie looks up at us both and smiles excitedly.

"And with the power invested in me, your mayor, I now pronounce you husband and wife, so help me God. You may kiss the bride." Garrett closes the Bible and lowers his head, and Maisie rolls her eyes. I take my new wife's chin and direct her lips onto mine.

"Happy now, Mrs. Hudson?" I ask her.

"Yes." She manages a smile, but only for a second.

"Okay then, let's have a baby." I move the cushions that are behind her outta the way and slide into their place so she can take both my hands, and rest back against me. When her next contraction comes, she bears down and I feel her whole body tremble from how hard she pushes.

"That's so good, the head's crowned," Maisie encourages her, and when Savannah joins her down the business end she looks equally as excited by what she's seeing.

"Keep pushing, Everleigh, you're doing great," one of them encourages her.

"Ya hear that? It's nearly over," I whisper when she takes a break to catch her breath and leans her head back against me.

"Oh God, another one's coming," she moans, closing her eyes tight and pushing hard against the next contraction.

"Yes, you're doing it! Hey, who needs a midwife?" Maisie calls out, and Garrett must get caught up in the excitement because he decides to have a peek at what's going on himself.

"Hey," I call out to him, "back up this end."

"Women are incredible." He shakes his head as he steps back toward the door.

"Everleigh, the whole head's out now, we just got to get past these shoulders, push really hard with the next one." Savannah strokes her leg and when Everleigh nods to say she's ready, I grip her hands tight and hold my own breath while she pushes.

I hear Garrett talking on the phone but I'm too focused on Everleigh and what's happening to care.

"That was Tate. The midwife's showed up at the ranch, he's pointed her in the right direction. I'm gonna go and meet her, make sure she finds her way here." I nod at him gratefully before he shoots off.

"This is it, one more big push, and your baby will be here," Maisie tells her, almost sounding like she knows what she's talking about.

"C'mon, darlin', you got this," I tell her, wanting all this to be over for her.

Everleigh's body goes rigid and she screams out as her nails dig into my hand, and when we hear the sound of a tiny, little cry we both breathe the same sigh of relief.

"It's here." Savannah looks up at us both with tears in her eyes. While Maisie wraps our baby up in a towel and passes it up carefully to Everleigh.

"You've got a beautiful, baby girl," she tells us as I look down at the beautiful, pink little person, who's crying her lungs out and instantly floods my chest with love.

"She's perfect." I kiss Everleigh's cheek as I offer my little girl my pinkie finger, and she immediately latches onto it like she needs me.

"You did it, look at her."

"I'm gonna leave this situation for the midwife, she can cut the cord when she gets here." Maisie moves away and Savannah and Leia follow her to the door. "We'll leave you two alone for a minute." She beams at us both before she closes the door.

"Look at the state of me." I use the hand my little girl ain't holding to wipe away my tears.

"We've got a little girl." Everleigh looks up over her shoulder at me.

"We've got the most *beautiful*, little girl in the world," I correct her.

"I love you," Everleigh tells our daughter, crying and laughing at the same time. Knowing that I played a role in the happiness she's feeling makes my chest feel like it'll burst.

"I love you too." She looks up at me again.

"You're incredible." I kiss her sweaty forehead and wrap my arms a little tighter around them both.

"Now, we just need to come up with a name for her." I open up the towel she's wrapped in so I can get a full look at her. She's long and has perfect little toes.

"Hope." Everleigh smiles down at her.

"Hope," I test out the name on my tongue and like how it sounds.

"I think that's perfect."

I cover my little Hope back up with the towel to keep her warm and kiss her mom's cheek, then I look up at the ceiling and thank God for that phone call I got from Jimmer Carson, asking for a favor.

Want to find out what happened when Savannah went into labor at the rodeo?

Sign up for my newsletter to get your free bonus scene by scanning the QR code below.

OTHER BOOKS BY EMMA CREED

The Dirty Souls MC Series: Colorado
0.5. **Bound Soul** (Freebie)
1. **Lost Soul**
2. **Reckless Soul**
3. **Vengeful Soul**
4. **Damaged Soul**
5. **Forbidden Soul**
6. **Untamed Soul**
7. **Tortured Soul**
8. **Stolen Soul**
9. **Captivated Soul**
10. **Abandoned Soul**
11. **Ruined Soul**
12. **Tarnished Soul**
13. **Broken Soul**
14. **Condemned Soul**

The Dirty Souls MC Spin-Off Series - Utah
1. **Empty Soul**
2. **Destined Soul**
3. **Rekindled Soul**

The Dirty Souls MC: Long Beach
1. **Raze**

Coming September 27, 2024
(Pre-order Link)
2. **Wrath**

THE CORRUPT COWBOYS SERIES

DUET #1
1. **Off Limits**
2. **No Limits**

DUET #2
3. **Testing Limits**
4. **Breaking Limits**

DUET #3
5. **Pushing Limits**
6. **Reaching Limits**

CORRUPT COWBOYS STANDALONES
Finding Limits

STANDALONES

His Captive
His Sacrifice

ABOUT THE AUTHOR

Come find/stalk me on the following social media platforms.

Facebook Group
Facebook Page
Twitter
Instagram
Goodreads
TikTok

Made in the USA
Monee, IL
04 March 2025

13423052R00146